"I'm sorry if I brou
memories tonight," Noah said.

"It's okay." Marti assured.

He smiled. "Great date, huh?"

"You do know how to show a girl a good time."

Noah tilted her face ever so slightly upward as he leaned in and met her mouth with his. Her arms went around him. His hand moved from her face to cradle the back of her head as his mouth opened even wider over hers. His tongue plundered and claimed and made her his, kissing her until nothing existed but the two of them and that kiss that drew her in, absorbed her and breathed new life into her all at once.

Dear Reader,

Noah Perry might have grown up a member of one of Northbridge's most well-known and respected families, but he made some bad choices of his own and learned that the consequences could be tough to take. Yet from that he decided to make himself a better man. Marti Grayson grew up with the love of her life, never thinking that it could come to an abrupt end when she least expected it and lay her lower than she ever thought she could go. And then one night Marti and Noah crossed paths and they saw the best in each other and got carried away by it, thinking never to see each other again.

But there were consequences of that, too, and when the pregnant Marti goes to the lovely little town of Northbridge and looks up from a dizzy spell to find Noah again, everything changes for them both. Change isn't always easy. But this time around, I think it might be worth it. I hope you think so, too, and enjoy this entry in the FAMOUS FAMILIES group of books that I'm proud to be a part of.

Happy reading!

Victoria Pade

VICTORIA PADE
A Baby for the Bachelor

SPECIAL EDITION®

Published by Silhouette Books

America's Publisher of Contemporary Romance

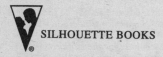

SILHOUETTE BOOKS

ISBN-13: 978-0-373-65453-6
ISBN-10:   0-373-65453-7

Recycling programs
for this product may
not exist in your area.

A BABY FOR THE BACHELOR

Visit Silhouette Books at www.eHarlequin.com

Printed in U.S.A.

VICTORIA PADE

is a native of Colorado, where she continues to live and work. Her passion—besides writing—is chocolate, which she indulges in frequently and in every form. She loves romance novels and romantic movies—the more lighthearted the better—but she likes a good, juicy mystery now and then, too.

Chapter One

"Wake up, Marti. I think we're close and I need guidance."

Marti Grayson opened her eyes at the sound of her brother's voice and sat up from her slump against the inside of his car door.

"Sorry. I wasn't much company, was I?"

"None," Ry said good-naturedly. "You fell asleep two miles from Missoula and you've been out ever since."

"That's been happening a lot lately. I'm told it comes with the territory—pregnancy hormones or something," she said before focusing her attention outside of the vehicle. "Northbridge?" she asked.

"That's what the sign said. But you tell me, you're the one who's been here before."

"For one night, three weeks ago. I got in late that Monday afternoon and left Tuesday morning."

Still, as Ry drove down Main Street in the small Montana town she recognized it as the street she'd driven in—and out—on.

"Take a right when you get to South Street," she instructed. "Gram's house is the last one before South Street goes out into farm- and ranchland. The driveway veers up a steep hill to the house."

In mid-April their elderly grandmother had escaped her nurse and surprised everyone by making her way to Northbridge. Theresa Hobbs Grayson had been born and raised there. The three grandchildren who made sure she was cared for in her mentally and emotionally unstable state hadn't known about the town or the house before that. But because Theresa was determined to remain there now, her grandchildren—Marti, Ry and the third triplet, Wyatt—were accommodating her.

Wyatt had been the first to come to Northbridge after Theresa was discovered in the old abandoned house. The plan had been for Marti, Ry and Wyatt to rotate spending time there with Theresa. But when Marti had arrived to relieve Wyatt, Wyatt had suddenly decided he wasn't leaving. He was going to relocate permanently in order to marry the local social worker who had been Theresa's case manager with Human Services.

Marti had needed to do a fast turnaround to get back to Missoula and the headquarters of Home-Max—the chain of large home-improvement stores owned by the Graysons. She'd had to take over for Wyatt there and so had not seen anything of Northbridge except what she'd driven through.

Now Wyatt was about to marry Neily Pratt and so both Marti and Ry were making the trip.

Ry had followed her directions and the house came into view in the distance. "Is that it?" he asked.

"That's it," Marti confirmed.

"It's a lot bigger than I thought," he said of the stately stone house that stood a tall two stories.

"I told you it was," Marti said. "The inside is good-sized, too, but barely livable."

"Who's that?" Ry interjected as they got closer. "Not Wyatt."

The house had a wide covered porch that ran the entire front and wrapped around one side to stretch all the way to the rear. Near the corner of the wraparound there was a man hanging a wooden bench seat that hung from chains.

His back was to them but Marti couldn't help noticing that it was quite a back—he was wearing jeans and a white T-shirt so tight it might as well have been painted on his V-shaped torso and shoulders that were a mile wide and extremely well muscled.

"That must be the contractor Wyatt hired to work on the place," Marti said, taking in what was undeniably an impressive view—especially when she factored in the narrow waist, tight rear end and long, thick legs.

"Noah Perry—isn't that his name?" she went on. "I never got a chance to meet him. The remodel and update is no small job, though, and now with the wedding this weekend Wyatt said they're in a crunch to have at least enough of the downstairs finished to be presentable. He said this Perry guy is putting in a lot of hours."

"Looks okay from out here."

Looks better than okay, Marti thought before she realized Ry was talking about the house while she was thinking about the contractor's butt.

And she shouldn't be thinking—or looking—at the contractor's butt. She pulled her gaze away.

"I still can't believe he's getting married again," Ry said.

Apparently not looking at the contractor wasn't enough to erase him from Marti's mind because for a split second she thought Ry was talking about him. Then she yanked her thoughts back in line and realized her brother was referring to Wyatt.

"How hard is this wedding gonna be on you?" Ry asked with a sidelong glance at her.

"It's okay," Marti assured him, appreciating his concern. "I've made this huge decision in my life in order to move on and that's what I'm going to keep reminding myself. Wyatt is having a new beginning, I'm having a new beginning."

"Huh, and I thought you were having a baby," Ry joked as he pulled into the driveway.

He turned off the engine and Marti stretched. It had been a long drive and she'd been sitting in one position the whole way. The stretch made her head spin slightly, though, and she stopped to take a deep breath. So far pregnancy was making itself known in extreme fatigue, more trips to the bathroom, some nausea and sudden bouts of dizziness.

Her head settled down after the third deep breath and she reached for the door handle as Ry got out of the driver's side and headed around the front of his newest toy.

The sports car was so low to the ground Marti had to duck a little to get out before she could stand and wave to Wyatt, who had come out of the house to greet them. And on came the whirlies again. Much worse than in the car.

Everything started to spin and tilt. Her gorge rose, and she felt herself sway uncontrollably. Her knees buckled and down she went like a helium balloon that had just lost all its oomph.

She heard both Ry and Wyatt call her name in a panic and come running. She wanted to reassure them that it was nothing, but beyond shaking her head she didn't have the wherewithal for more.

Deep breaths... Deep breaths... It'll pass...

Her brothers were on either side of her by then, asking if she was all right, but it was as if their voices were coming from far away, and all she could do was sit there, bracing herself with one arm to keep upright while her head was in some sort of internal spin.

Another man chimed in, in a voice that was vaguely familiar although Marti couldn't place it. He was suggesting they call for an ambulance.

"No!" she managed as she struggled not to lose her lunch.

"Mary Pat!"

That was Wyatt's voice, yelling for her grandmother's caregiver. Mary Pat must have already been on her way because a moment later the nurse was kneeling beside her, taking her pulse.

"It's just…dizziness…" Marti whispered as the wave finally began to subside. Then she said, "I'm okay. Really."

Embarrassment inched in behind the dizzy spell when she heard Ry say, "Maybe this artificial insemination thing wasn't such a great idea. I'm not so sure pregnancy agrees with you."

"Ry…" Wyatt chided. "Filter it, will you?"

"I'm just saying—"

"It doesn't need to *be* said. Especially not out here on the lawn."

With some stranger standing there, Marti thought as she put all her efforts into regaining herself.

She swallowed hard, closed her eyes for a minute and took a few more deep breaths before she repeated, "I'm really okay. I just keep getting this wicked dizziness thing."

Then she opened her eyes and looked to her other brother, appreciating that he had the sense to curb Ry's lack of discretion, and smiled feebly.

"Hi, Wyatt," she said as if nothing had separated his greeting and that moment.

"Hi, Marti," Wyatt said, alarm in his expression but his tone calm and understanding.

Marti looked to her grandmother's caregiver. "Hi, Mary Pat. Could you tell these guys there's nothing to this?"

"I think she's fine," the nurse confirmed. Then, to Marti she said, "Do you want to try to stand or shall we sit here a few minutes?"

"Why don't we see if I can't actually make it to the house." Truthfully she *would* have preferred to stay put, if only everyone—including the handsome stranger—would stop staring.

"Here, let us get you up," Wyatt insisted as he took one arm and Ry took the other.

That just made Marti feel like more of a spectacle. "I'm not an invalid, you know, guys."

Neither of them commented, they just helped her to her feet.

And that was when her gaze went to the other onlooker—the man who had been hanging the chair swing on the porch and had obviously rushed down to her rescue along with her brothers.

"This is Noah Perry," Wyatt said. "Noah, this is my brother Ry and our sister Marti."

And that was when Marti swallowed hard a second time.

"Actually," Noah said in a deep, rich voice she suddenly remembered all too well, "Marti and I have already met. At the Hardware Expo at the end of March."

So she wasn't hallucinating.

She'd almost hoped she might be.

"That's right," she confirmed weakly, not knowing what to do or say as her head started to spin for an entirely different reason.

While she hadn't recognized the man from the back, now that she was face-to-face with him, she didn't need an introduction. She knew that wavy chestnut hair, that slightly hawkish nose, those lush lips, those rich brown eyes. They'd been haunting her thoughts for the last six weeks.

"You better get inside, your color is draining again," Mary Pat said, hooking her arm into Marti's. "Come with me. I'll get you some water and maybe a little sugar pick-me-up."

Marti still hadn't found any other words to say and Mary Pat was urging her to move so she just went, her thoughts on the man she'd thought she'd never see again.

The man who was the *real* father of her baby.

An hour after the late-afternoon excitement with the Graysons, Noah Perry went home to a Friday night full of plans to pry off baseboards in his living room and possibly start to paint the walls.

Before he did either of those things he took some carrots and a cold longneck beer out of the refrigerator and went to his back porch to enjoy the warm mid-May evening and say hello to Dilly.

The three-year-old female donkey came over to the porch railing the minute Noah stepped outside.

"Yeah, you know what I have for you, don't you?" Noah said to the animal as he gave Dilly one of the carrots.

He had two more but rather than give them to the

burro right away, he put them in his pocket and leaned a shoulder against the post that braced the porch roof. Then he sipped his beer and did what he'd been doing for the last hour—he marveled at the fact that he'd just met up with Marti again. That she was Marti *Grayson*...

Last names hadn't come up at the Expo. Sure, he'd known she worked for Home-Max—he'd seen her manning their booths and in their hospitality suite. But there had been Home-Max employees all over the place, and he'd just figured she was in their ranks. She hadn't said she was one of the *owners* of the chain.

And in the three weeks he'd been working for the Graysons, there hadn't been any mention of Marti by name or he might have put two and two together. On the occasions when he'd talked to Wyatt—or on the fewer occasions when he'd talked to Theresa—there had only been occasional mentions of "my sister" or "my granddaughter," never a name. So he honestly hadn't had a clue.

He *had* been weighing whether or not to ask Wyatt about the Marti who worked for Home-Max, though. He just hadn't made up his mind if he should.

Sure, he'd had trouble not thinking about her in the last six weeks. Who wouldn't have? She was just damn gorgeous. She had long blond hair, shot through with lighter streaks of pure sunshine, falling to the middle of her back. She had the softest, smoothest, most flawless skin he'd ever seen—or touched. Her eyes were the dark silver-blue of his first car and her lips were the reddest, fullest, sweetest he'd ever kissed. And her body was just round enough, just full enough in the right spots, just lean enough in the rest. And it was all atop surprisingly long legs for someone who didn't stand more than five feet four inches tall.

So yeah, he'd had trouble not thinking about her and even dreaming about her a time or two.

But he hadn't inquired about a Home-Max employee named Marti because he'd been asking himself where it would go even if he did find out her full name or how to reach her. She'd told him she worked and lived in Missoula. He worked and lived in Northbridge— Missoula was on the other side of the state. And a one-night hook-up at a hardware convention was hardly enough to work from. For all he knew, an almost anony-mous, one-night fling was all she'd wanted. Certainly the fact that she'd left the next morning without waking him to say goodbye or so much as scribbling him a note seemed to indicate that.

But damn, what a night it had been!

The Hardware Expo had been a chance for him to get away for a weekend and keep himself updated on the latest products and all things construction related that might make his job as a contractor easier. But that was the extent of what he'd been looking for. It wasn't as if he'd been cruising for women.

Still, he'd noticed Marti more than once—how could he not have when she was such a knockout? They'd ex-changed a little work talk in passing at the Home-Max displays. They'd spoken slightly more when he'd gone to the hospitality suite, and yes, his interest had been piqued by something other than the latest cupboards and countertops. But she'd been busy, he'd been interested in a lot of things at the convention and nothing had come of any of it.

Then, late on the last night of the Expo, they'd both happened to be in the nearly deserted coffee shop in the hotel where the convention had been held.

He'd nodded at her.

She'd nodded back.

He'd said hello.

She'd said hello back.

And there they'd been—Marti alone at one table, Noah alone at another table, only waitstaff and a single group of other customers in the entire rest of the place.

So Noah had invited Marti to eat with him.

And she'd accepted.

More small talk about hardware had accompanied two club sandwiches and despite the fact that the conversation was work related, there *had* been a few flirtatious undertones from them both. And when the check had come Noah hadn't been eager to see her go.

So he'd asked her if she might like to have a nightcap with him at the hotel bar.

She'd hesitated long enough for him to have figured she was trying to find a way to let him down easy. But just when he'd been sure he was about to get the rebuff, she'd said a nightcap sounded good.

The bar had had live—and loud—music that had prohibited talking. So they had ended up dancing. And drinking. A lot. Enough so that when the bar had closed neither of them had been feeling any pain and not actually knowing each other just hadn't seemed to matter. He'd felt comfortable with her. He'd sure as hell liked looking at her. The evening had become one of the best he'd ever had, and a playful kiss in the elevator had somehow led her to walk him to his door when they reached his floor.

A good-night kiss there had turned into a whole lot of good-night kisses. Good-night kisses that had moved from the hallway to the inside of his room, then to the bed.

Where a lot more than kissing had gone on…

Noah fed Dilly another carrot. "To tell you the truth," he confessed to the donkey as if the animal had been privy to his thoughts. "I wish I remembered it better than I do. The details of things, you know? But I was *really* drunk…"

They both were.

So drunk that when things between them had gone pretty far and he'd told her he didn't have any condoms, they'd stupidly decided to risk it…

Noah had forgotten *that* detail completely.

Now that it occurred to him—struck him, actually—everything seemed to stop cold.

He hadn't used protection…

And now here she was, six weeks later, pregnant…

"Oh my God!" he said, loudly enough for Dilly's ears to twitch.

No protection and now Marti was pregnant—it went through his mind again, sinking in enough for his mouth to go dry, for him to break into a sweat.

Her brother had said it was by artificial insemination, he reminded himself. Until that moment that's what he'd assumed was true, and maybe it was.

But as much as he wanted to believe it, it didn't seem likely. Had she spent the night with him, had unprotected sex that *hadn't* gotten her pregnant and then decided to try artificial insemination? Somehow that was hard to buy.

But what if she'd already been pregnant at the Expo? What if knowing she was already pregnant had contributed to her willingness to forego the condom?

Okay, that *did* seem possible.

Possible enough to give him a little hope and let him at least breathe again.

"It might not be mine," he said out loud even though Dilly was keeping her distance.

But it might be—he couldn't help coming back to that. Especially when he factored in that Marti had been every bit as drunk—maybe more drunk—than he'd been. And if she'd been pregnant before that night, she probably wouldn't have touched alcohol…

"Oh my God," he said again. Marti Grayson wasn't just a beautiful, hazy memory of a faraway night in a rustic hotel room at a hardware convention, but a flesh-and-blood person with brothers and a grandmother and who-knew-who-else to contend with and save face with by saying she'd gone to a sperm bank rather than admitting she'd had a one-night stand with a stranger and gotten pregnant.

But if he was the father of her baby, why hadn't she come looking for him to let him know?

"Did I tell her I was from Northbridge?" he asked Dilly as if the donkey might know.

Truthfully he couldn't remember. And if all he'd said was that he was from a small town in southern Montana and she hadn't known his last name, she probably wouldn't have been able to find him. Maybe it was only by some greater design or coincidence that they'd been brought back together after she'd done everything she could to locate him.

Or maybe the baby was his and she didn't want him in on it so she hadn't bothered to even look for him...

But thinking that just made things worse.

Was she another woman who wasn't going to give him a say or any options as a father? Because if she was, that just wasn't going to fly.

Sensing the anger that flooded through him then, the donkey backed up a few steps.

"It's okay, Dilly. It's not you," he comforted the animal, offering the third carrot to make amends.

The burro came cautiously forward, keeping her big black eyes on Noah and getting only close enough to reach the carrot.

"It might not be mine," Noah said once more in an attempt to calm the emotions that had him reeling. "But I'll have to find out one way or another."

Because if the baby *was* his, he was going to have to do something about it.

Something that could keep the past from repeating itself—again.

Chapter Two

Later that night, after Marti heard Theresa's bedroom door close, she said to Wyatt, "How is she doing?"

"Gram?" Wyatt shrugged. "No better. No worse. She had a bad night last night. The nightmares have been happening on a regular basis and usually with that same theme—she says *it's* crying for her, *it* won't stop crying, she has to get *it* back."

"Which is why we're thinking *it* is not the land she wants back," Ry contributed.

Since Theresa's escape to Northbridge, Wyatt had been looking into their grandmother's past there. What he'd learned so far was that Theresa's parents had died when she was a young girl, and that Theresa had inherited the house and many acres of prime property in the heart of Northbridge. Because her only other relative—an aunt—had been ill and unable to take her in at the time, Theresa had spent eleven months after the deaths of her parents as the houseguest of local lumberyard owner Hector Tyson and his wife Gloria.

During those eleven months she'd had virtually no contact with any of her friends, and at the end of them—three months before her eighteenth birthday—she'd finally left Northbridge to live with her aunt in Missoula. Before she left she sold Hector Tyson her land for a quarter of its value. Hector Tyson had subsequently become wealthy dividing the land into lots, selling those lots, then selling all the building materials to erect the houses that now stood on them.

When Theresa had been discovered three weeks ago in the house where she'd grown up, she'd been demanding that what had been taken from her be returned. Originally Wyatt had believed she'd been talking about the land. But since the nightmares had begun—and since Theresa had dismissed the notion that this had anything to do with the land—her grandchildren had started to wonder what else she might be referring to. If it might even have been a baby she'd had by Hector.

"Which is why we're not thinking it's the land that she wants back, right," Wyatt repeated what Ry had said.

"And why it seems like *it* might be a baby," Marti said, summing up what they'd all touched on through recent phone calls. "But you still haven't asked her straight-out if that's what was taken from her?"

Wyatt shook his head. "It hasn't seemed like a good

idea. She's been in one of her really bad funks—she's weepy, withdrawn, disoriented. Her memory has been worse than usual—she even forgot who Mary Pat was last week. Today—knowing you two were coming—is the first really good day she's had since that first nightmare."

"And you still haven't talked to this Hector Tyson?" Ry asked.

"He's been out of town this whole time. I understand he gets back on Monday, so it looks like it'll be up to you, Marti. Ry will be on his way to Missoula right after the wedding to take care of business there, and I'll be on my honeymoon. Do you think you can handle it?"

Marti knew her afternoon dizzy spell had them thinking she couldn't but she wasn't about to accept that. "Of course, I think I can handle it," she said as if it were ridiculous for him to ask. Then, because she wanted them to know that everything should be business as usual, she returned to the subject of their grandmother. "And Ry, you have a meeting with the lawyers to see if there are any legal options for restitution from the sale of the land, right?"

"Right," Ry answered.

"Then you and I will take it from here while Wyatt lies on the beach," she concluded.

Her brothers exchanged a glance that she would have been able to read even if they weren't triplets and inordinately in tune with each other.

"Knock it off," she ordered.

"Knock what off?" Wyatt asked.

"This whole can-I-handle-it, is-Marti-all-right thing.

Because I *am* all right. Yes, Jack's death hit me hard. Yes, maybe it's a little over the top to decide to have a baby on my own. But seriously, I'm okay."

"You didn't look okay sitting on the ground this afternoon," Ry said, never one to mince words.

"Dizziness—no big deal. I also sometimes throw up if I so much as get a whiff of breakfast sausage—it just comes with the territory." That seemed like something Wyatt would know, since his first wife had been pregnant when a household accident had taken her life and the life of the baby. But she didn't say that. Instead she said, "I've been to the doctor, I'm healthy as a horse, the baby is doing fine and having it is a sure sign that I'm moving forward. That I'm putting Jack's death behind me."

"It took Wyatt two years after Mikayla died to give in to his feelings for Neily," a clearly concerned Ry put in. "It's only been nine months—"

"Nine and a half, actually," Marti corrected.

"Okay, nine and a half months since you lost the guy you'd been madly in love with since you were both kids," Ry persisted. "The love of your life, Marti. The guy we *all* thought was your other half. Come on, if you were in our shoes, wouldn't you be worried that you're acting out of some kind of grief mania and maybe not thinking straight or handling anything well?"

"I know how it looks," Marti said calmly. "It looks like I've gone a little nuts. But I haven't. In spite of the dizziness and the rest of the pregnancy annoyances, I feel good about this baby. I feel better than I've felt since Jack died and I can't believe that's anything but positive, so that's how I'm going to look at it. If you have qualms—"

"Keep them to yourself," Wyatt advised.

"I was going to say get over them, but that's good, too," Marti said. "And as for staying in Northbridge a while to be with Gram, and checking out the site Wyatt found for the new store here, I'm as capable of doing all of that now as I was before I was pregnant. End of discussion!"

Neither of her brothers looked convinced. They both just sat there with worried expressions on their faces.

"I appreciate that you guys care. I really do. But I haven't gone off the deep end. It was just meant to be that I have a baby at this point—with Jack or without him," she said, pushing on to get through this. "Yes, it's sad that it isn't Jack's baby or that he isn't here to have it with me and make up the family we thought we'd have…" She took a deep breath to steady herself. "But that doesn't mean there's anything wrong with this new path. It's just a new path."

And with that she couldn't possibly have said another word on the subject without breaking down. So she stood and said she was tired and was going to bed.

She'd made it to the bottom of the stairs when she heard Ry say to Wyatt, "I told you, ever since the Expo she's been different."

Marti pretended she hadn't heard and went up the creaky old stairs, maintaining her air of confidence until she was behind the closed door of her current bedroom.

The first floor was beginning to show signs of improvement and after the wedding Marti intended to move into the downstairs den. But until then she was staying upstairs in what had been her grandmother's room as a girl, and almost nothing had been done to that. While the room was clean, it showed its age in the canopy bed that was missing its canopy due to decay, an ancient, scarred bureau and matching dressing table and a large cheval mirror that was cracked in one corner.

Marti went to the bed and collapsed in a heap, letting a long sigh deflate that phony facade she'd been keeping up for the last few days since she'd invented the artificial insemination story for her brothers. The facade she'd had to kick up a notch since that afternoon when yet another curveball had been tossed at her in the form of Noah Perry.

"Am I the only one you can knock around?" she muttered to whatever unseen forces seemed to be at work in her life for the last nine-and-a-half months.

Regardless of how she was presenting everything to her brothers, underneath it all she was a wreck.

She'd hoped never to go through anything more stressful than the death of her fiancé. But the last few weeks had rivaled it.

Pregnant. She'd done one dumb thing in her life and had she been allowed to just get away with it? No. She'd gotten pregnant!

It wasn't as if she'd planned to go to Denver that last weekend in March and sleep with a stranger. It wasn't as if it had even crossed her mind. She'd volunteered to oversee the Hardware Expo just to escape for a few days.

To escape the constant reminders of Jack everywhere she looked, everywhere she went, every which way she turned. To escape all the well-intentioned sympathy and pity of friends and family. To escape the awkward position of being a sort-of-but-not-really widow.

She'd just wanted a few days without anyone tiptoeing around her or being overly solicitous of her. A few days of not needing to assure everyone she spoke to that she was okay. A few days to interact with people who didn't know her or Jack or what had happened. People who were just going about their lives the way they always had.

Which was exactly what she'd found and for the whole three days of the Expo she'd felt as if at least half of the weight on her shoulders had been lifted. It had actually been easier to endure the bouts of grief without all the coddling and fussing.

Bouts of grief—she realized as she thought that that's what the grieving was becoming. That it wasn't the constant, ever-present entity that it had been at the beginning. That now she was doing what Wyatt had said she would—that the times when she felt better and more able to cope, more as if she really was going to get through it, were increasing. That the times when she was blinded by it were becoming fewer and further between.

And the Expo had helped that along.

And so had Noah Perry...

She'd encountered him on several occasions over those three days. Not that she'd known his name. Until the night in the coffee shop he was just another face among the gazillion faces that had passed through Home-Max's displays or visited the hospitality suite.

And yet here she was, having his baby.

Overwhelmed by that all over again, she lay on her side on the bed with her feet still on the floor.

The image of Noah's face had stuck with her at least, she thought in a feeble attempt to somehow make this seem less awful than it did. He *was* memorably handsome, though. Which was why she'd noticed him even among the crowd at the Expo and amid a sea of other faces in the suite when he'd passed through.

He had rugged good looks—a sharply defined bone structure that gave him a square brow, high cheekbones, a razor-sharp nose and a jawline that was strong and prominent.

But it was his hair and eyes that had really stuck with her. There was nothing common or ordinary about them.

He had great hair. Dark and thick and wavy. And although he wore it a little longer than she'd liked Jack to wear his, it suited this guy. Full and carelessly combed away from that chiseled face, it touched his collar in the back and gave him an untamed, bad-boy air.

And his eyes—they were the color of melted bittersweet chocolate, shining and penetrating and patient. Eyes that looked as if they had intelligence behind them. That seemed to see past the surface.

She'd already thought that if her baby was born with its father's hair and eyes it would be beautiful…

But she hadn't just taken one glance at the man and

said, "take me, I'm yours," because he looked good…
well, better than good, great. Still, that hadn't been
enough for her to spend the night with him. No, that
had come out of a combination of things, including
a few cocktails too many and an apparent weakness
for the cute guy she'd repeatedly seen around the trade
show.

Would she have agreed to join him for a bite to eat
if her inhibitions hadn't already been compromised?

Probably. Because in a way, by then the man she'd
been thinking of for three days as The Cute Guy had
become a part of the reason she'd gone to the Expo in
the first place. He'd treated her normally.

He'd joked with her. He'd been friendly. He'd been
funny and charming and clever. And yes, he'd even
flirted with her a little.

Not that she'd *wanted* someone to flirt with her, but
when he had, it had felt good. It had also felt good to
discover that she could even flirt back—something she
hadn't known she could do with anyone but Jack. So
she'd opted to allow herself one last brush with that
before returning to reality in Missoula and had had a
sandwich with The Cute Guy.

And she'd enjoyed herself.

Yes, she'd felt guilty. A part of her had felt as if she
were being unfaithful to Jack.

But like her brother Ry, Jack had always been about
living life, about grabbing it and shaking every last drop
out of it. He'd said again and again after Wyatt's wife
had died that the living had to go on living. He'd even

said that if anything ever happened to him, he wanted Marti to jump right back on the bandwagon, that he didn't want her wasting any time wallowing.

Easier said than done.

Maybe her less-than-sober state that night in the coffee shop had also been a factor, but when The Cute Guy had asked her to go to the bar for a nightcap and she'd debated whether or not she should, in her mind she'd heard Jack's voice urging her to go ahead…

So she had.

She'd gone to the hotel bar for more drinking. Some dancing. For some fun.

And when it should have been over, she hadn't wanted it to be…

That was the last clear thing she remembered. The rest was far, far more fuzzy. A complete blur, actually. The kissing. His room. His bed. Clothes coming off in the dark. Letting herself just go with feeling good, with what she wanted at that moment…

The next thing she'd known, morning sunshine was coming in through the windows, she wasn't drunk anymore and she was appalled by what she'd done. So she'd dressed in a silent hurry and slinked out of his room.

She hadn't told a soul about that night and the further she'd gotten away from it, the more she'd begun to see it merely as something that had helped her turn a corner in her grieving for Jack. And she'd viewed that as a good thing because it had made her realize that she *was* going to survive losing him, that she just might be able to go on without him after all.

And then she'd missed her period.

For a few days she'd told herself it was just late, that it would start any minute.

For a few days after that she'd told herself there could be any number of reasons to miss a period— stress had caused her to miss the first one after Jack's death.

By the time she was two weeks late she'd bought a home pregnancy test. When it had come up positive, she'd rushed to her doctor, hoping it was a false positive.

It wasn't.

Shock, horror, fear, panic—she'd gone through them all since then. But when she'd been able to calm down and think it through, she'd decided that maybe the pregnancy, and the baby, were signs that she really did have to push on. To go forward. To leave the past behind. And so she'd decided to do just that. By having the baby.

She'd considered how she might track down The Cute Guy whose name she thought was Norm. She didn't know anything about him other than he was a contractor from somewhere in southeast Montana and what floor of the hotel his room had been on. Still, those were starting points and she'd thought she might be able to use them to persuade the hotel to give her his full name and address. But for what? she'd asked herself.

She didn't need financial help. She had no idea who he really was or what his background might be, or if he might have a family. She had no idea what kind of damage could be done if she pursued him with this, or what sort of reaction or response she'd be met with. So it just seemed better to leave things the way they were. To consider the baby hers and hers alone, to have it and raise it on her own and to leave the-Cute-Guy-from-the-Expo none the wiser.

So she'd concocted the artificial insemination story.

And even if it wasn't true, she still liked the message it gave—that she'd taken control of her life again and was moving forward, albeit unconventionally. Plus, since telling her brothers and a few friends the tale and presenting it as something she'd actively gone after and achieved, it almost felt as if that's what she'd done.

Then she'd looked up into the face of The Cute Guy again that afternoon...

Since then, relief was certainly not what she'd been feeling.

She rolled onto her back, flung her arms wide and let out a huge groan.

"What am I supposed to do now?" she asked the heavens.

No answer was forthcoming.

But seeing Noah again changed things and she knew it. She was going to have to rethink what to do from here.

"Only not right now. Tomorrow," she said to herself, shying away from it because at that moment it just felt like more than she could deal with. Besides, wasn't it better to wait to think about it all after a night's sleep?

Of course it was. Especially when she was too tired to even trade the sweats she'd put on after her post-travel shower for pajamas or move up to the pillow.

Tomorrow was another day.

And who knew? Maybe she'd wake up and she wouldn't be in such a mess.

Chapter Three

Saturday was hectic. There were last-minute wedding preparations for Sunday evening's ceremony, rearrangement of the furniture to accommodate the reception, decorating to be done, deliveries of food and flowers and tables and chairs and other necessities. There was the rehearsal and the dinner, and the introduction of Neily's sister, five brothers and their spouses and dates to Wyatt's family.

Because of the commotion at the house, Noah Perry's work on the remodel was suspended for the weekend. And while he wasn't a member of the wedding party and so wasn't included in the rehearsal or the dinner afterward, he was still on Marti's mind almost constantly through Saturday and Saturday night. All without coming to any better conclusion than she had on Friday—she needed to do some fact-finding before she decided how to proceed.

Then Sunday evening came, and guests finally began to arrive for the seven o'clock ceremony.

Once Marti had carefully styled her hair in a French twist, applied her makeup and dressed in her curve-hugging, short black dress, she stood at the window of her upstairs bedroom watching for Noah. And trying to make her stomach stop doing somersaults at the mere thought that she was going to see him again.

He arrived early because he was providing the transportation for his grandfather, who was the former town reverend and was performing the ceremony in the absence of the current, vacationing, minister. As Noah helped the elderly man get up to the house, Marti couldn't keep from taking stock of her baby's father.

Noah had been dressed casually at the Expo and he'd been in work clothes on Friday, but now he was wearing a navy blue suit over a cerulean blue shirt and a darker blue tie. The suit fit him so well he could have been an endorsement for the good tailoring to be found in North-bridge—his broad shoulders filled the jacket to perfection before it tapered to just hint at his narrow waist, and the pants whispered down long, long legs to break exactly where they should.

His hair still had that devil-may-care look to it, off-setting the clothes any Wall Street executive would have been proud to wear, and combined it made for a picture Marti just couldn't take her eyes off of.

But tonight is just about getting some background in-

formation, she reminded herself of the only thing she'd come up with after two nights of not very restful sleep and a full day of consideration in between. She was going to take things in small steps, hoping that way she could handle it better and arrive at a rational, intelligent, best-for-everyone plan of action.

When it came time for the ceremony it was Ry who persuaded the agoraphobic Theresa to go down the back stairs and into the kitchen with Mary Pat where she could watch Wyatt and Neily say their vows without seeing or being seen by any of the guests.

Because Wyatt had wanted both Ry and Marti to be his grooms-people, as he called them, Neily had chosen her sister Mara and oldest brother Cam to give balance to the attendants. Standing with her brothers, her back to the onlookers, Marti wondered if Noah Perry was watching her the way she'd watched him on his way into the house. And just assuming that he might be did not help those stomach somersaults one bit.

His grandfather performed a stern but gracious ceremony that only lasted twenty minutes, and when it was over, Mary Pat slipped Theresa back upstairs to her bedroom and the reception began.

That was when Marti lost all awareness of anything or anyone other than Noah Perry, whose gaze was definitely trained on her as she congratulated Wyatt and Neily.

Noah didn't approach her, though. He just kept an eye on her as the music began to play and guests started to mingle. And even when she caught him watching her, he didn't cover it up by glancing away. He just went on looking at her, studying her, until she pretended that something else had caught *her* attention.

Go on, go over and talk to him, she told herself.

But instead she went upstairs to make sure her grand-mother wasn't too agitated in the aftermath of her foray to the kitchen.

The food was being served buffet-style and by the time Marti returned almost everyone was eating. Only a few stragglers were going through the line and Noah was at the end of it.

Maybe now's the time, she thought. After all, she could step up behind him, fill a plate and say hello—belatedly, but exactly as she had with everyone else tonight. Then maybe she could nonchalantly sit with him to eat and use small talk to get into her fact-finding mission to learn about him before she made her decision as to whether or not to admit the baby was his.

So why didn't she budge?

Because she was a great big fat chicken!

Maybe he didn't really want to know if the baby was his, she thought. After all, he hadn't made a beeline to her to ask—he could have come to the house just to see her yesterday if he was dying to know, and even tonight he could have cornered her immediately after the ceremony.

Or maybe he was obtuse and it hadn't even occurred to him that the baby might be his. Maybe he'd accepted the artificial insemination story at face value. Maybe she could just go on the way she'd planned even though their paths *had* crossed again...

Or maybe not. Because when he reached the end of

the serving table he turned to look out over the room, spotted her and headed toward her.

Marti was inclined to run again. To make a dash for the stairs and take refuge in her grandmother's room as if she hadn't noticed Noah's beautiful brown eyes locked onto her with single-minded intent.

But she didn't run. She forced her feet to stay planted right where they were. She breathed deeply. She told herself to act as if nothing was going on. She even managed a small smile—although she cut that short when she felt her lips quiver nervously.

"I took enough for two," he said when he reached her, motioning upward with his plate. "I thought maybe we could share."

Then he leaned in and said for her ears only, "If we can share that night in Denver, we can share a plate, can't we?"

Openly referring to that night sent a wave of panic through her. "I'm not very hungry—"

"Sit with me anyway," he countered, not allowing her any out.

Oh, he's suspicious, all right...

But this was something she needed to do and he'd just initiated the process for her. She knew she had to push through, so she conceded, nodding over her shoulder at the entryway behind them. "Want to sit on the steps?" she asked hesitantly.

"Sure."

It was quieter in the entry, away from everyone else gathered in the living room. Marti went to the large staircase that rose to the upper level and sat on the second step, hugging the wall so Noah could sit, too, but not too closely.

He took the hint, positioning himself at an angle with his back to the newel post. Then he set the plate on the step between them and handed her one of the two forks and two napkins he'd brought.

"I took some of everything since I wasn't sure what you might like," he said then, stabbing a small parsley-buttered potato for himself.

As he ate, he looked at her again the way he had been all through the evening, as if he were cataloging what he remembered and what he didn't.

Marti pretended to be more interested in the cherry tomato she was trying to skewer than in him.

"How are you today?" he asked.

"Fine," she was quick to assure him. "That was just a little dizzy spell yesterday. I'd been sitting in the car for so long and it was low to the ground and I got up fast—" That was all more information than he needed and she cut herself off before it went any further and said, "Today I'm fine," and popped the tomato into her mouth.

Noah continued to look at her for a moment after she'd stopped babbling. Then, in a completely conversational tone, he said, "So. Pregnant, huh?"

He was definitely suspicious.

"Mmm-hmm, pregnant," she confirmed as if it were no big deal. But that was as far as she was willing to go and she volleyed with, "So. Northbridge, huh?"

His agile mouth twitched with a tiny smile at her deflection but she had the distinct impression that he was going to let her set the pace, that he wasn't going to force the issue. And he didn't. Instead he merely said, "Northbridge, yeah. Born and raised."

"You didn't tell me that in Denver, did you? Didn't you just say that you were from a small town in southeast Montana?"

"I think so. I didn't think you would know Northbridge by name. Would you have?"

Marti shook her head. "No. I'd never heard of it before Gram showed up here."

Noah glanced in the direction of the bedrooms on the upper level. "You couldn't get her to come down tonight?"

"She was hidden in the kitchen during the wedding itself but not even Ry could get her to do more than that—and if anyone can ever talk her into anything, it's Ry. She keeps saying she can't face anyone here, that she's too ashamed, but we don't know what that means."

Noah nodded and ate a bite of ham, again leaving the ball in her court.

Marti knew that while talking about her grandmother might seem like a safe subject, it wasn't getting her the information she needed. So she didn't take it any further, seizing something she hoped might. "The reverend is your grandfather?"

"Yep," Noah confirmed. "For better or worse."

"Why for better or worse?"

"He's a tough old bird—so tough that not even the family dare to call him anything but Reverend. He's not the most understanding or compassionate or forgiving person in the world."

Was there a message in that? Was he saying that he was more understanding, compassionate and forgiving than his grandfather? *And what exactly did he think he had to be understanding or compassionate or forgiving of?* Marti thought, feeling a tweak of her temper.

It wouldn't do her any good to get angry, though, she told herself. So she didn't pursue that either, and instead, as if she hadn't seen his arrival for herself, she said, "Did you only bring your grandfather tonight?"

"Who else was I supposed to bring?" Noah asked.

Marti shrugged. "Your wife…"

That made him smile and she knew he understood exactly what she was doing. But all she could think about was that it was a thousand-watt smile with perfect, straight, white teeth. A smile that put creases down his cheeks. A smile she remembered now that she'd seen it again, that transformed his face from handsome to striking. A smile that got to her more than any other smile she'd ever seen, including Jack's.

"*Now* you're asking me if I'm married?" he said.

His smile broadened, making her grin sheepishly in response.

"I don't recall you asking me, either," she accused in return.

"Are you?"

"No. Are you?"

"No," he said.

At least there was that. Marti felt a miniscule sense of relief.

"What about a girlfriend or a significant other?" she asked.

"Nope. You?"

Marti shook her head and took one slice of bread from the plate, breaking off a pinch to eat and wondering if the next question she wanted to ask would open a door she wasn't ready to have opened.

But she honestly did want to know who could be affected by her pregnancy if she told Noah he was the father, so she said, "How about kids? Do you have any of those around?"

He'd been looking down at the plate when she said that and while he didn't raise his head, he did glance up at her from beneath his slightly full eyebrows. "No, no kids either," he said with some gravity. And maybe the tiniest bit of a question in it, too.

Or was she only imagining that?

She couldn't tell. And there he was talking again so she let it go.

"I do have a brother and two sisters, if you're interested in my family tree. And three cousins—they're sitting together over by the fireplace," he said, pointing toward the far side of the living room where a group of people had convened at one of the rented tables. "That's all of them except my sister Kate. She's out of town and couldn't come. And my parents and my aunt and uncle live in Billings now."

He leaned slightly toward her to continue in a more confidential tone, "I also have a grandmother we've all just met—Celeste. She's pretty notorious. She caused a huge scandal by ditching the Reverend to run off with a bank robber. See the heavyset lady sticking close to Neily's sister Mara? That's my grandmother and this is the first time she and the Reverend have been at the same social event in years. So if all hell breaks loose between them sometime tonight, you've been forewarned."

Marti had to smile again at that, remembering that he could be very amusing, too.

"Wow, the whole family," she said. "Skeletons in the closet and everything—nothing like putting it all out there."

"I'm an open book," he assured her, eating a forkful of green salad. "Ask me anything."

Marti broke off another bite of the bread because that was the only thing she'd eaten that wasn't threatening to upset her stomach. Food and nerves just didn't mesh. And while talking to Noah like this again was reminding her why she'd been attracted to him in the first place that night in Denver, she was still on edge and undecided about what she was going to do about him, and that was making her queasy.

"Are you close to your family?" she asked, taking him up on his offer to tell her anything.

"Most of them are right over there—how much closer do you want us to be?" he joked.

"I know people who *seem* to be close to their families but aren't. Just because you live near them—"

"No, I don't just live near them. I like them, too. I'd run into a burning building for any one of them and they'd do the same for me." He said that as if he truly meant it. Then he looked at her very intently, pinning her with those eyes of his as he added, "Family is important to me. Really, really important."

Uh-oh...

Marti could see in his expression and hear in his voice where he was going with that. And she just didn't know if she was ready for it. If she could be honest with him. If she should be. She didn't have any more idea of where things might go from here than she had when they'd sat down, or if she should let him in, or what kind of havoc might be wreaked if she did.

It's my baby, she suddenly wanted to make perfectly clear to him. *Mine...*

But before Noah seemed able to find the words to ask outright, his grandfather appeared from the living room pounding his cane on the hardwood floor to gain their attention.

"Noah!" the Reverend said, his voice booming despite his frail, spindly appearance.

Noah's gaze remained on Marti for another moment before he turned to his grandfather. "Reverend," he answered, sounding none too happy to be interrupted.

The old man didn't seem to care. "I'm tired. Take me home," he demanded.

"Could you give me a minute?"

"No! I want to go now!"

Noah sighed, obviously knowing the Reverend would have his way or else. "Okay."

Marti watched as Noah grabbed his grandfather's

topcoat from the hall and helped him pull it on, her gaze fixed on Noah's strong hands, recalling how they'd cupped her shoulders and let her feel their power in the most enticing way…

But thoughts like that had no place at the moment. She told herself that she should just be glad the old reverend had bought her a little more time to think through what she was going to do instead of being distracted by her attraction to Noah.

Embracing her reprieve, she stood to join the two men at the door to see them out.

"Thank you for the lovely ceremony, Reverend," she said politely to the elderly man, despite his rude attitude.

In response he grumbled something she didn't quite catch as Noah opened the door for him and he went out.

Noah didn't follow him immediately the way Marti thought he would. He paused a moment to look at her, to let those dark chocolate eyes delve into hers once more.

Then, in a low voice that was again for her alone to hear, he said, "Is it mine?"

Panic shot through Marti stronger than before and a thousand thoughts ran through her head.

But the only one that stuck was that while she might not know much of anything about this guy, she knew he was nobody's fool.

"Is it, Marti? Is the baby mine?" he reiterated after his grandfather had made another demand from outside to be taken home.

Please don't let this turn out badly…

"Yes," she whispered, still not sure it was the right thing to do.

Noah's gaze dropped for just a split second to her middle, then rose to meet her eyes again.

He didn't say anything. He merely stared at her a minute more, his brows beetled together in a dark, dark frown.

Then he nodded—really only a raise of his chin in acknowledgment—before he followed his grandfather out of the house.

Chapter Four

Noah was a no-show for work on Monday. He didn't call. He didn't send any kind of message saying he wouldn't be there. He didn't respond to the voice mail Wyatt left when Wyatt called to ask where he was before Neily and Wyatt left for their honeymoon.

"It'll be fine. I'll deal with it. It isn't as if I haven't handled contractors before," Marti assured both of her brothers so Ry could get on the road to Missoula, too.

But underneath it all?

Marti was even more of a wreck than she'd been before.

She just didn't know *why*.

So what if Noah had freaked out about the baby? So what if he didn't want anything to do with her or the pregnancy or with his child once it was here? She hadn't intended to make him a part of it before this, she'd intended to do it on her own anyway.

What difference did it make if he'd ended up knowing? It didn't change anything. The baby was still hers. She was still going to have it, raise it, love it. If he didn't want any part of that, fine, she told herself.

Absolutely fine. No problem whatsoever. All the better, probably.

Yet, for some reason, thinking that that was the reason he'd done a disappearing act today had thrown her off balance, and by the end of Monday afternoon she just wanted to get away from everything to have a moment to herself.

So she trudged up to her bedroom, feeling the weight of all she'd found in Northbridge bearing down on her. Wondering if she really could do what she'd convinced her brothers she could when it came to the conundrum surrounding Theresa, and taking the next steps in opening a new Home-Max in the small town and overseeing the renovations of the house by the contractor who had gotten her pregnant and now made himself scarce...

No, it was okay that Noah seemed to have vanished into thin air, she told herself again as she closed the bedroom door and pressed her forehead to it. At least nobody else knew he was the baby's father. At least nothing on the surface had changed.

And if she'd gone to bed last night thinking about those deep, dark eyes and that smile that could spread out so slowly it was like waiting for Christmas and a voice as rich as hot fudge? Well, now she knew how Noah had gotten to her in Denver, but it didn't have anything to do with here and now.

Here and now the fact of the matter was that Noah was not Jack—Jack who would have been thrilled with a baby, who would have marveled at every minute of the pregnancy they shared, who would never have left her hanging—and she needed to make sure she didn't lose sight of that.

But yes, today she felt as if she was carrying a pretty heavy load on her shoulders, and despite her show of strength and confidence and invincibility to her brothers, she was feeling anything but.

The house phone rang just then and Marti held her breath, hating that everything seemed to pause as she waited to hear if the call might be from the sexy contractor.

And then Mary Pat yelled up, "It's for you, Marti. It's Noah," and in that split second the dark clouds over her head seemed to part.

But that wasn't good, either, she cautioned herself.

"He's probably just calling to say he's history when it comes to the baby *and* the remodel," she muttered.

But if that was the case, she needed to get it over with so she would know exactly where she stood and could just get on with this new twist, too.

So she hollered back to Mary Pat, "I'll be right there," and pushed away from the bedroom door to open it.

As she retraced her steps downstairs to take the call

there sprang to life a tiny ray of something she tried to ignore.

Something that felt a little like the hope that underneath Noah Perry's laid-back charm and simmering sensuality she might find that he was a stand-up guy after all.

Marti arrived at the coffeehouse earlier than she'd told Noah she would be there. That had been the purpose of his phone call late in the afternoon—to ask her to meet him for coffee that evening. He hadn't apologized for not coming to work, nor had he said anything about the baby. In a very serious, sober tone of voice, he had merely told her he wanted to meet with her. And she'd agreed.

Then she'd skipped dinner because her stomach had been too tied in knots to put food in it. Instead she'd taken a second shower, shampooed her hair and carefully chosen a pair of low-slung brown linen slacks and a cream-colored silk sweater set. She'd caught the sides of her hair in a clip in back and left the rest of it to fall free, added mascara, blush and a little lip gloss to finish her efforts, then drove Wyatt's SUV to Main Street and the small establishment that served hot and cold beverages and a few pastries.

And there she was, trying to prepare herself for whatever was about to come her way. Anticipating the worst.

She didn't have long to wait. Noah arrived five minutes after her. The front of the place was all windows so from her seat at a corner table where her back was to the wall, she saw him drive up.

He parked his white truck at the curb and got out. Marti couldn't be sure, but she had the impression that he might have put some thought into his own clothes. He had on a pair of dark denim jeans and a tan V-neck sweater over a white crew-necked T-shirt. There wasn't even the hint of a beard on his handsome face so she knew he'd shaved right before he left.

Looks can be deceiving, though, she thought when she couldn't help the twinge of appreciation for the sight he presented. No matter how good a presentation he made, if he was there to tell her what she thought he was there to tell her, he was a creep.

He spotted her the minute he walked into the place and came over to her. "Hi," he greeted her simply with a tight-lipped impersonation of a smile that was clearly wary.

"Hi," she answered just as guardedly.

"Thanks for coming."

Marti nodded.

"What can I get you?" he asked with a glance over his broad shoulder toward the counter where orders were taken. "Can you drink coffee? *Do* you drink coffee?"

We don't even know that about each other, Marti lamented.

"I'll have a decaf nonfat latte."

"I'll be right back," he said as he left again.

Marti watched him at the counter, unable to deny that the rear view was almost as good as the front because his jeans encased a derriere too prime not to notice.

Then he turned with their coffees and she quickly raised her gaze to his ruggedly striking face again.

When he reached the table, he set one of the two cups in front of her and kept the other in hand as he sat across from her.

Marti tasted her coffee and waited—he'd asked for this meeting, it was his show.

"I'm sorry about not working at the house today," he began. "And for not answering the voice mails."

Marti merely nodded.

"I had a lot of thinking—and some other things—to do after…the news I left with last night."

There was nothing to be said to that so she just went on waiting.

"I don't…" he began, stopped, restarted. "It occurred to me when your brothers said you were pregnant Friday that I could be…the cause. Not right away—I was actually slow on the uptake. But then I realized that it was a possibility. So I don't know why it hit me like a ton of bricks last night when you said the baby is mine, but it did."

"It has a way of doing that," she allowed conservatively.

"I paced the floors most of the night and then today I went to see my lawyer—"

"Your *lawyer?*" she repeated, cutting him off as her mind started to race again.

Was he going to demand proof? A paternity test? What exactly was he implying about her? And if he had proof, would he be willing—reluctantly—to concede to being this baby's father?

"Look," Marti said then, ire echoing in her tone,

"until I just happened to meet you again on Friday, I fully intended to do this on my own. I don't want anything from you. I don't need anything from you. If you want to tell yourself this baby isn't yours, if that makes it easier for you, then be my guest. As far as I'm concerned—"

"Whoa, whoa, whoa," Noah said in an angry tone of his own to go with the dark frown on his handsome face. "Who said anything about me wanting to think it isn't mine?"

"Isn't that why you went to a lawyer? To force some kind of paternity test in hopes that you *aren't* the father?"

"That didn't even cross my mind. Should it have?"

"No. There have only been two men on my dance card—the man I should be married to right now and you."

That had probably not been the best way to put that and the minute the words were out, Marti regretted them. This was all just so hard and complicated.

But Noah didn't seem to take offense. In fact, he did the opposite—his temper seemed to recede and in its place he became conciliatory.

"I'm not questioning whether or not the baby is mine. The timing is right. I don't remember a whole lot about that night but I do remember that we were drunk enough to take the risk of not using protection. You'd already told that artificial insemination story to your brothers—I don't think you would have done that if the father was someone you know or were involved with. And another one of the few things I recall is you saying more than once that night in Denver how that wasn't something you'd ever done or ever did—and that struck me as true. Plus, while I don't know much about you, what I've seen doesn't make me think that you're someone who would try to pass off someone else's kid on me."

Apparently he thought higher of her than she'd been thinking of him in the last several hours. It helped Marti to calm down slightly.

"Thanks for that at least," she said. "And I didn't faint on Friday, it was—"

"I know, it was a dizzy spell," he said with the first hint of a genuine smile—and it *was* only a hint. "But when I saw you go down I thought you'd passed out."

They both sipped their coffees and after a brief pause, Marti said, "So why *did* you go to a lawyer today?"

"To find out what I needed to do to protect my rights."

"Your rights?"

"As the father. I'm not trying to figure a way *out* of this, Marti. I want to make sure I have a firm footing *in* it."

That surprised her.

And then it alarmed her. In her wildest dreams she hadn't thought there was any risk of the father of this baby doing anything that might take it away from her in some fashion.

"What does that mean?" she asked in a quiet voice.

"This is a big deal to me," he said with enough gravity that she didn't need any more convincing to believe he wasn't taking this lightly. In fact, he said it with so much gravity that it made her wonder if there was more motivating him than she knew.

But he was still talking and this was all too important for her to let her mind wander.

"I realize that I'm as responsible for this as you are," he was saying. "And I'm not one of those people who can ignore that I'll have a kid floating around out in the world and just go on about my business as if I don't. There's no way I'd let you go through this alone, and once the baby is here, I want to be a father to it. I want to be a part of its life."

"Okay…" Marti agreed with reservation because she still wasn't sure exactly where he was going with this. "What did you have in mind?"

"First of all—I want to know that you aren't going to have an abor—"

"No," she said firmly. "I'm having the baby."

"Great." Noah looked relieved.

"And second of all?" she said.

His face broke into a bigger and even more genuine smile. "As long as there *is* going to be a baby, second of all becomes first of all—I'd like it if we could back things up and get to know each other."

"And you need a lawyer for that?"

"I wasn't sure if I should try to get something in writing—like a custody agreement that would guarantee that I could be a part of things. But I was in the lawyer's office, going through possibilities in that direction and everything he was asking me seemed to set such a hostile tone. That's not what I want, Marti. Not for you or for me or for the baby. So I thought maybe we could go at this another way and start where we should have started before."

So he wasn't talking any of the extremes her imagination had taken her to—he wasn't turning his back on her and fatherhood, and he wasn't thinking about making some kind of power play to take her baby away from her.

And yet she still felt compelled to say, "That's it— just get to know each other?"

"That's it. For now. We have nine months—"

"Seven and a half."

"We have seven and a half months, and then, when the baby is here, we can hash through it from there."

That was slightly unnerving—she hadn't even had the baby yet and she didn't want to think about shared custody or visitation or anything else he was talking about.

But seven and a half months was a long time, she told herself. And he was right, the best first step was for them to simply get to know each other. She would deal with the rest when the time came. For now it just helped that he *was* proving to be a stand-up guy. And the fact that he was taking his share of the responsibility for the baby, that he was treating it like something he *wanted* to be included in, helped it seem more like what she'd been trying to see it as since she'd decided to go through with it—an unplanned pregnancy that could be looked at for its positives rather than its negatives. And handled with some dignity. And she was grateful for that.

Besides, deep down Marti had to admit that a tiny

part of her was relieved that she wouldn't have to go through this completely on her own. Because as much as she knew she could depend on her brothers, there was only so much she knew she could ask of them.

"Okay," she said, not realizing until she had that a long silence had passed while she'd thought things through.

"Okay?" Noah repeated hopefully.

"I think you're right, us getting to know each other does make sense at this point. And I'm in Northbridge for a while, you're working on the house, we'll be right under each other's noses—what better time?"

He looked immensely relieved and she knew at that moment that he'd come there tonight with his own concerns. And again she had the sense that whatever those concerns were, they weren't unfounded, she just didn't know what they were founded on. Maybe that would come with getting to know him.

"Thanks," he said then.

Marti laughed a little. "For what?"

"For accepting that it's my baby, too."

That increased her feeling that his fears of being shut out were connected to some event in his past. But it was too soon to probe so she merely said, "Well, thanks for owning up to the baby being yours."

That made his smile grow into a grin. "You really did think the worst, didn't you?"

"I kind of did," she confessed.

"Bad experience?"

"No!" she was quick to respond in pure reflex to defend Jack.

"So it was just me you thought was a jerk?"

"I didn't know what to think," she admitted. "This isn't a position I've ever been in before and, well, you know, you hear a lot of variations on how the father reacts. I guess I just went with the lowest expectations. It seems like one of those situations that can bring out the worst in people."

"Or the best," he suggested.

Once more she liked that he was taking the positive over the negative and she wondered if he always did that. She supposed she would find that out about him, too.

But not *right* now because they'd both finished their coffees and it had been a long twenty-four hours. Marti was feeling drained and when Noah asked if she'd like a refill she declined and told him she thought it was time for her to get going.

Noah walked her to Wyatt's SUV and made sure he was positioned to open the unlocked driver's side door for her.

But she didn't get in immediately. She thanked him and stood in the lee of the open door to face him. "You don't happen to know a man named Hector Tyson, do you?" she asked.

"Sure. He owns the lumberyard and the only thing that passes for a hardware store around here. I know him well."

"Is there any chance that you could introduce me?" she asked.

"I'd be happy to," he answered. "Is this about Theresa selling Hector the land she inherited from her parents when she was a girl?"

So he knew that, at least. Wyatt must have told him. Or working on the house had made it impossible for him not to overhear some of what had been going on with her grandmother. In any event, Marti saw no reason to be evasive when uncovering secrets was her goal.

"Yes, it's about Gram," she answered. "We have a lot of questions for this Tyson guy, but Wyatt said he's been out of town."

"He has been. But he's back now."

"I need to see him, but I hate to just ring his doorbell and pummel him with questions like a census taker."

"No, that wouldn't go over well. I don't know if anybody's told you about Hector but it's a toss-up as to who's more of a contrary old cuss—Hector or my grandfather. And you met my grandfather so you know what I'm talking about."

"Not a warm and fuzzy man," Marti understated.

"More like a human cactus. And Hector doesn't even have the whole righteous do-gooder thing going for him. He's just mean-spirited and greedy and pretty much all-around unpleasant."

"I can hardly wait to meet him," Marti said facetiously. "But I don't have a choice. We're trying to do whatever we can to help Gram and too many things track back to this Hector Tyson to ignore him."

Noah nodded in understanding. "Well, I can get you in and introduce you, but I won't be able to promise that it'll be a lot of fun. I could buy you a pizza afterward, though…"

Marti laughed. "Are you saying that it will be so bad

that there will be a need for stress eating and consoling afterward?"

Noah smiled again, that warm smile that had won him her time in Denver. "Probably," he confirmed. "But even if there isn't a *need,* I'm figuring I have to get in a full day's work tomorrow since I skipped today. So I'll try to persuade Hector to see us early in the evening. That way I can go home for a shower and a change of clothes. And once we're finished with him, it'll be dinnertime."

Since they were now committed to getting to know each other, dinner together might as well follow—simple, practical, convenient. Yet she was suddenly looking forward to it as if it were more than just pragmatic.

She opted not to look too closely at that, though, and to merely go with the flow of things.

"Pizza it is, then," she agreed, looking up at Noah in the light of a nearby streetlamp.

"Pizza it is," he repeated, gazing down at her in a way that gave her a flashback to that night in Denver.

It was nothing strong or vivid or at all clear. It was just an instantaneous image of standing facing him, of their eyes meeting, of him leaning forward.

Of him kissing her…

There were only the faintest of details, but in that moment she recalled being surprised by how much she'd liked the way he kissed. She recalled thinking that it had never occurred to her that anyone else's kisses could ever do to her what Jack's had.

But Noah's had.

And out of the blue came the wish that he *would* kiss her again, right then.

Just so she'd know what his kisses were like, she told herself. So she'd know if she was thinking that they were better than they actually were. If his mouth was as gentle and commanding. What she might—somewhere in the recesses of her brain—have a vague recollection of.

Kisses she'd liked more than she'd imagined possible. That had carried her away…

Oh great, that's just what I need—to get carried away again. Especially just for the sake of appeasing some kind of curiosity…

No, she told herself, there was no reason to wonder how the man kissed, let alone to check it out. Whether or not Noah's kisses were as good as Jack's didn't make the slightest difference. It wasn't anything she should care about.

"I'll set it up, then," Noah said.

It took a moment for his words to get through to her. He was saying he would set up the meeting with Hector Tyson.

And she needed to get her head back into the here and now…

"Thanks, I'd appreciate that," Marti managed, feeling like an idiot and doing everything she could to focus. "Thanks for the coffee, too," she added when she remembered that as well.

"You bet."

He was still looking down into her eyes, though. Why did he keep doing that?

As if he'd heard her thoughts, he did break eye contact, glancing at a couple walking by before he said to Marti, "I'll be at the house bright and early tomorrow so I guess I'll see you then."

Marti merely nodded and finally got into the SUV.

Noah closed the door for her and leaned toward the open window to say, "Drive safe."

Marti nodded and again had the inordinate urge to poke her face upward and have him kiss her.

Then it occurred to her, had Noah been Jack, that was what she would have done and maybe that was all that was really happening here—the pull of an old habit.

But as she started the engine, put the SUV into reverse and backed away from the curb under Noah's still watchful eye, she didn't feel as if she were in the throes of an old habit.

She felt a genuine pull toward Noah.

Chapter Five

"Yes, I would have known you were related to Theresa Hobbs just by looking—you're the image of her," Hector Tyson said to Marti after motioning for her to sit on the sofa across from the wing chair in his living room on Tuesday evening.

As promised, Noah had arranged to have the eighty-four-year-old man see them. Marti and Noah had been let into his impressive house by a housekeeper and shown to the living room where the elderly gentleman had remained seated as if on a throne throughout Noah's introduction of Marti.

Marti had heard through reports from Wyatt that Hector Tyson was supposed to have been quite a heart-breaker in his youth and shades of his earlier hand-

someness were still in evidence now. Despite the fact
that he didn't stand, she could tell by the length of his
legs and by his height in the chair that he was tall and
he held himself with straight posture. His shoulders
were still expansive, his body lean, and while his hair
had gone completely white, it remained thick and
lustrous atop a face that was deeply lined but still very
attractive.

"What can I do for you?" he asked when Marti had
taken the offered seat while Noah stood behind her and
to one side like a bodyguard.

Hector Tyson's attitude seemed somehow smug,
although Marti couldn't pinpoint why. He stared at
her with eyes that were still clear and alert and very
blue, and made her feel like a fly that had just unwit-
tingly flown into a spider's web. Obviously Noah
hadn't been exaggerating when he'd said the man was
unpleasant.

But in answer to his question about what he could
do for her, she made sure she was respectful.

"There are some things I wanted to talk to you
about," she said.

"What sort of *things?*" he asked, mocking her.

Matter-of-factly, Marti said, "My grandmother is insisting that we get back something that was taken from
her by you."

The old man chuckled mirthlessly at that. "Yes, I'd
heard that poor Theresa isn't quite right in the head.
What exactly am I to have taken from her?"

"At this point we're working from the assumption

that it was the land she inherited from her parents. The land you ended up with."

"Check the land records... Oh, that's right, one of you already did that, didn't you? So you know that I *ended up* with that land because I bought it from Theresa—fair and square. And at her request, I might add."

Wyatt and his new wife *had* checked the land records and there was nothing questionable about the sale. Except the price.

"Gram *asked* you to buy her out?"

"It was all her idea," Hector said, not in the least unnerved by what they were discussing. "My late wife Gloria and I took her in when she had nowhere else to go—her mother and father had died, and her only living relative was an aunt in poor health who couldn't have her move to Missoula immediately. But Theresa was the daughter of a friend and business associate, and my wife and I certainly couldn't sit by and see a young girl left unconsoled in her darkest hour of grief. We offered her a home and our support. But after several months—"

"Eleven," Marti supplied.

"After eleven months, when her aunt was well again, Theresa thought she might be happier away from Northbridge and the memories here, so she decided to go to her aunt."

"And sell you her land for a quarter of what it was worth?" Marti asked.

"She wanted all ties with Northbridge severed—completely and as fast as possible. When I told her that

I couldn't pay her market value for the property, she said she didn't care. That her father would have wanted me to have it in any event and so we struck a deal."

Marti thought that Tyson might not have Noah's grandfather's religious righteousness, but he seemed to have no shortage of self-righteousness.

"But if my grandmother wanted to severe all ties with Northbridge why didn't she sell the house, too?" Marti asked.

The elderly man merely shrugged. "I suppose you would have to ask her that question."

Marti wondered if it might be time to push another button and took into consideration that Noah was there, listening to everything. They hadn't discussed the more lurid suspicions of what might have happened between her grandmother and Hector Tyson, but when she'd spoken to Wyatt on the phone that morning he'd told her he had talked to Noah about Theresa and her past at length in hopes of garnering any morsel of information the Northbridge native might have. There was no reason for Marti to try to conceal anything from him now, she just hoped he didn't find it embarrassing.

"My brothers and I are also wondering if there might be something else Gram is talking about when she says you took it from her. Something of a more personal and emotional value to her," Marti said.

"Such as?"

"Were you and my grandmother…involved, Mr. Tyson?" Marti asked.

"Involved?" he repeated. "Do you mean romantically?"

"You weren't that far off in age—she was seventeen, you were twenty-six. We've heard that you were quite a ladies' man and that my grandmother might have had a crush on you…" Marti said, thinking to stroke his ego and at the same time let him know that there was some basis for the suspicion that he and Theresa might have had an affair.

Hector shrugged his arrogant eyebrows this time. "Yes, I believe Theresa did have some feelings for me. But I was a married man and loyal to my wife."

Noah cleared his throat and it earned him a scathing glance from Hector before the old man returned his gaze to Marti.

"I'm sure Noah will tell you later that I was not *always* faithful to my late wife, but at that time, early in the marriage, nothing went on between Theresa and me. She was a grieving young girl, I was merely someone who gave her a helping hand. And as for taking something from her—I certainly did nothing like that. I did only what she asked of me—I bought her land so that she would have the money she needed to leave town. And if, in the bargain, I ended up with a good deal, well, it suited both of our purposes."

And yet he was getting hot under the collar, Marti noted.

Hot enough to seem unable to contain himself because without provocation he added, "And I've been told that your grandmother is out of her mind. Deranged. That she can't remember what she's eaten for breakfast by the time she has lunch. I'm sure whatever it is she's talking about is some sort of delusion, and if what she's saying has anything to do with me or those months she spent here, it's nothing more than a figment of her imagination. I did a good deed—I took her in—and what do I get for my trouble? Accused of taking something from her and cheating on my wife?"

Marti refused to lose her temper with him even though his talking about her grandmother the way he was pushed buttons of her own. "For your *trouble* you got a lot of land for a quarter on the dollar."

"Count the rest as her room and board!" the old man sneered. "And I'll tell you something else, young lady," he continued. "I know what you Graysons are up to. I know you think you're going to bring one of your Home-Max stores to Northbridge to try to put me out of business. Well, I won't let it happen. That holding barn you thought you had locked up? Sold to me today at five o'clock! And getting to tell you that myself is the only reason I let Noah bring you here tonight—how do you like that?"

That was why he'd seemed smug from the start.

"The seller accepted our offer on that barn. It was under contract," Marti said, anger in her tone.

"And I outbid you by so much that the seller was willing to pay penalties to give it to me instead. You're not fooling with some weak, failing old man here, *Miss* Grayson. Or with a whiny lunatic like your grandmother. I'll stomp you people into the ground and you might as well learn it from the start."

"Is that what you did to my grandmother all those years ago? *Stomp* her into the ground?" Marti countered.

"Of course not!" Hector shouted venomously, defensively. "Your grandmother got what she wanted from me—the money for her land. No matter how she's crying about it now. Don't come around here talking to me about what I might have *taken* from her. I didn't have to *take* anything."

"That's about enough, Hector," Noah said, stepping forward and suddenly making himself a towering presence that halted the old man's rant.

By then Marti was too livid to know what to do or say, and she was glad Noah was there to take over.

"Is there anything else you want from him, Marti?" he asked her.

Staring daggers at the old man who gave the impression that he was savoring his victory over her, Marti shook her head.

"Then let's go," Noah suggested.

"That's right," shouted Hector. "Go. Go back to Missoula or wherever it is you came from. You'll never open a Home-Max in Northbridge, *Miss* Grayson—not if I can stop you."

Marti spent some time composing herself in the restroom of the pizza place shortly after leaving Hector Tyson's house. During the drive to the restaurant Noah had patiently listened to her tirade about the things Hector Tyson had said, but now she wanted to put the meeting behind her. After splashing cool water on her face, she finally felt calm enough to return to Noah. But one step outside of the restroom, one glance across the small restaurant to where he sat and she stopped to watch him.

He wasn't merely sitting waiting for her. He was standing, reaching across the table to build a pyramid of what appeared to be candy bars at her place setting.

In the midst of venting about Hector Tyson's unmitigated gall, she'd made the comment that after an encounter like that, she needed more than pizza to counteract the stress—mounds of chocolate were required, too.

And there was Noah, building her a mound of chocolate.

And looking indescribably appealing himself, in a crisp white shirt with the sleeves rolled to his elbows and his to-die-for, jean-encased derriere right where she could feast her eyes.

The sight made her smile in spite of herself as she crossed the restaurant just as he sat down.

"Is this my appetizer?" she asked when she reached him, nodding at the pyramid comprised of at least a dozen different kinds of candy bars.

"That's what you said you needed, that's what I got for you. After I ordered our pizza I sneaked into the general store across the street just as they were locking up and forced them to make one more sale."

"You already ordered the pizza, too?" Marti asked as she took her seat.

"The specialty of the house—everything but anchovies. I just thought that after Hector, I'd better pull out the big guns when it came to stress eating and consoling."

Her words from the night before. It made her smile again.

"I just wanted to punch that man!" Marti said, unwrapping a package of peanut butter cups and taking a bite.

Noah grinned. "I can't believe it—you're really eating chocolate *before* dinner?"

"Hey, you bought it. Besides, this one has peanut butter in it—that's protein."

"I thought you were kidding about eating candy instead of pizza. I bought them as a joke."

"That'll teach you."

"Give me the rest of that before you polish it all off," he pretended to chastise, moving the remainder of the candy bars out of the way as she ate the second peanut butter cup. "You can't feed my baby candy."

"I can. And I do. I can't have wine, but I can have chocolate and it's a good thing—wine I can go without, but never, ever, chocolate!"

He tossed another bar on the table in front of her the way a zookeeper might throw a steak to a ferocious lion. "Do what you need to," he said.

Marti laughed and slid the candy bar back. "I'm okay for now," she assured. "But I still can't believe what that man said about my grandmother, and that he bought that barn out from under us. You weren't lying when you said he was a horrible person."

"Through and through."

"How could Gram possibly have *ever* had a crush on him?"

Noah shrugged. "Hector's never had a shortage of female company, believe it or not. There was a long line of women that he cheated on his wife with. Apparently when it suits his purposes, he can show different colors."

"And getting Gram to sell him that land obviously suited his purposes," Marti muttered. "But I wasn't going to talk any more about that," she added to remind herself.

Aiding that cause, their pizza arrived. It was almost as big as the table itself and piled high with toppings. The waitress served them each a slice before leaving them to eat.

"I feel the stress draining away already," Marti joked after her first bite.

"Good?" Noah asked.

"Wonderful," Marti answered honestly.

"That's a relief—after I ordered it I wondered if you had any weird pregnancy cravings or if there were things you couldn't stand to eat or smell or something. I've heard that can happen."

"Eggs," she said, almost gagging on the word.

After another bite of his slice, Noah said, "So, dizzy spells and the unmentionable food—is pregnancy causing any other problems for you? Morning sickness or anything?"

Marti smiled again. "I sleep a lot," she said. "More than I ever have in my life. But I'm told that's normal."

He shrugged one of those broad shoulders. "I

couldn't say one way or another. But you've seen a doctor, right? Everything seems okay?"

"I've seen a doctor—twice already—and yes, everything so far is fine."

"And you're...at peace with being pregnant, having a baby?"

"At peace?" Marti asked, confused.

"Do you have doubts or regrets? Do you hate that this has happened? Do you feel like you've completely accepted it..."

It was a strange question and, like talking to him the night before, she had the sense that there was something behind it.

"Are you worried about that?" she asked.

"Sure," he said as if anyone would be.

Maybe they would be, Marti thought, giving him the benefit of the doubt and deciding to simply answer his question.

"I can't say I don't have any regrets—this isn't a situation anyone wishes herself into. Or one I ever thought I'd be in. But yes, I'd say I've completely accepted it and no, I don't have doubts about my decision to have the baby. It's...well, it's a step forward for me—that's how I'm looking at it. An affirmation of life. When moving forward and having something life-affirming to make that happen was what I needed."

But getting any more deeply into that would mean getting into her own baggage and she wasn't ready for that. So she turned the tables on him and said, "What about you? Doubts, regrets, hate that this has happened?"

He didn't seem to need to think about that—or maybe he already had—because he shook his head as he finished the bite of pizza he was working on and then said, "I'm with you—not an ideal situation. But the most important thing now is just to make the best of it. And I want you to know that I'm here for you—anything I can do, anything you need, all you have to do is say the word."

He'd made that apparent when an offhand remark had netted her a slew of candy bars.

It was sweet of him, though. And nice to have someone offering what she would have expected of Jack had she and Jack gotten to this point.

"So you'll keep me in chocolate?" she teased.

"A constant supply," he promised.

"That might require a second job."

"Maybe I can get one with Home-Max when it opens."

"*If* it opens now that we don't have a site," Marti said.

"There are other empty buildings around here. I know someone who wants to sell a section of storefronts right on Main Street. He hates Hector so much he'd never sell to him. He'd probably be more inclined to sell to you just to spite Hector. You could look into knocking down walls to combine the space. And I'm great with knocking down walls, so *that* could be my chocolate job."

"Problems solved all the way around," Marti joked again. "But seriously, will you put me in touch with the owner of the storefronts?"

"Tomorrow." Noah took his second slice of pizza and said, "Is that part of your job for Home-Max—procurer of property?"

"That sounds bad—like I'm the property pimp," she said with a laugh. "But no, not necessarily. Ry, Wyatt and I share all jobs pretty equally, including finding a site or land to build on when we decide to open a new store."

"Have you always been into hardware?"

He'd clearly intended that one to have a double entendre and Marti laughed.

"Always," she said emphatically, playing along.

"As a little girl you wanted hammers and pliers instead of dolls?"

The innuendo was gone with that and Marti realized he was genuinely interested.

She didn't mind. "No, as a little girl I was all girl— I had dolls and an amazing playhouse and I tormented the dog by putting her in dresses."

"Even with two brothers, you weren't a tomboy?"

"I could hold my own with them, too. I went through bicycle tires faster than either Ry or Wyatt because I rode so hard. I could pitch a baseball better than either of them. And they learned early not to mess with me or they'd get back twice as much grief as they dished out."

Noah grinned at that notion. "I'll bet you got away with more because you were the only girl, too—in my family our parents always thought my sisters were the innocent victims even when they weren't, just because they were girls."

Marti smiled. "I admit I took some advantage of that. Once in particular, when my brothers dared me to put a lit cherry bomb in the refrigerator to see if it would go off in the cold. I blew up the whole inside—food and all—and ruined a nearly new fridge. Since they had the cherry bombs to start with, they got the blame and they still haven't let me live that one down."

Again Noah grinned at her story. "Other than that, did you get along with your brothers when you were kids?"

"Oh, yeah. Maybe it's the triplet thing—you did know we're triplets, didn't you?"

"I'd heard."

"Well, triplets or not, I don't know any siblings who were closer than we were, and still are. We worked together in the family hardware stores when we were kids and hung out with each other. We work together now, live near each other in Missoula, we even take vacations together when we can. And we're always there for each other—good times and bad."

"*Have* there been bad times?"

He was definitely fishing, but she still wasn't ready to let him get to know *that* much about her, so she said, "Gram's mental health issues are bad. Wyatt's wife and baby dying—that was bad. And I've had some bad of my own. But as I said, we get through everything together."

Noah nodded, seeming to concede that she wasn't going to give him more than that yet. Then he said, "So how PO'd are your brothers going to be at me when they find out that I'm actually responsible for getting their unmarried sister pregnant?"

"I'm not sure," she said frankly. "Truthfully, even the artificial insemination idea didn't go over all that well—

you probably noticed that on Friday. Wyatt is trying to keep his feelings more under wraps than Ry—Ry has always been more outspoken. But when I told them that story they both sort of…recoiled. So neither of them is comfortable with it. I guess it's possible they could be happy to find out I made that up. But the whole one-night stand with a stranger thing? That's going to shock them. They know that just isn't like me."

And she wasn't looking forward to telling them. Especially not since they'd loved Jack almost as much as she had. She wasn't eager to see how disappointed they were going to be to find out that she'd slept with someone else—someone she hadn't even known—eight months after their best friend's death…

Noah must have sensed her dread of telling her brothers because he said, "Would it make it easier on you if we come up with a story? Like that we met a long time ago and have been secretly seeing each other?"

"That would actually be worse and there's no way they'd believe it," she said without telling him why. "On the other hand, they might be understanding," she allowed then, considering some of the unlike-himself behavior that had come out of Wyatt's grief and the fact that Ry and Marti had both been through it with him and not held it against him. Maybe they wouldn't hold this against her.

"I guess it's just hard to say how they'll react," she said, getting back to Noah's original question. "Wyatt seems to like you, though—that doesn't hurt anything."

"Do you have plans for when to tell them?"

"Just when it seems opportune. And it's probably better to tell them when they're together."

Noah nodded again. "I'll leave it up to you whether or not you want me to be with you when the time comes. I can take the heat if you do, so don't let that be a factor."

"You think you can take on both of my brothers at once?" she teased him again.

Noah didn't take the bait, though. He just smiled, unperturbed by the possibility of her brothers' anger but showing no bravado—two more things that appealed to her.

But she reminded herself that they were there to get to know each other, not to find anything appealing or attractive, so she tried to curb it by taking her eyes off of him to push away her plate.

"I think you overestimated how much pizza I can eat even under stress," she said with a glance at what remained of the enormous pie.

"It's great left over. And cold. For breakfast."

Marti didn't know why, but the pizza she'd enjoyed only moments before suddenly looked very unappetizing. All that sausage and pepperoni and salami and cheese and those shriveled vegetables and congealing grease…

"Okay, maybe I'm having a problem with eggs *and* the idea of cold, leftover meat for breakfast," she said, making a face to go with her queasy stomach. "You'd better take it."

"You could reheat it."

"That's okay," she assured him, trying to wash away

the nausea with a drink of water, looking anywhere but at that pizza in front of her and trying not to breathe too deeply so she couldn't smell it.

"Not too okay," Noah said then. "You're looking a little green around the gills."

"I think I ate more than I should have," she managed weakly and only after swallowing hard.

"Maybe we should get you home."

"Maybe we should. Maybe I should wait outside," she added, grabbing her purse and making a dash for the door and some fresh air.

Through the windows at the front of the restaurant Marti saw Noah call their waitress over to box the remainder of the pizza. While the waitress was doing that he put the candy bars in the bag he must have gotten when he'd bought them. Then he paid the bill and came outside.

"Are you all right?" he asked, sounding concerned.

"Better," she said because it was true—her stomach was beginning to settle. "But I don't think I can be anywhere near that pizza."

"No problem," he said, setting the box in the flatbed of his truck before opening the passenger door for her.

"Sorry," she apologized when he'd closed her door, rounded the truck's front end and joined her to start the engine and pull away from the restaurant.

As they drove down Main Street he pointed out the empty storefronts he thought she might be interested in for Home-Max, and that also helped to get her mind off her stomach. Before she knew it they were back at her grandmother's house and she felt fine again.

"Let me walk you all the way inside," Noah offered as they neared the front door.

"That's okay. The wave has passed. I'm even considering another candy bar before bed," she told him in a voice steady enough to be convincing.

He handed her the bag and didn't insist on going inside. But as they stood facing each other in the glow of the porch light he studied her as if he wasn't sure whether or not to believe her.

"Really, I'm all right. It was just some pregnancy weirdness. No big deal," she insisted.

"I've never seen anybody look so sick so fast."

"Pregnancy weirdness," she repeated. Then, to get him off the subject, she said, "Thanks again for taking me to meet Hector Tyson."

Noah smiled wryly. "You're thanking me for taking you to meet someone who gave you a hard time and insulted your grandmother?"

"I am. I needed to touch base with him, and now that I have I know what we're dealing with. And it was good that you were there as backup when he attacked."

It occurred to her suddenly just how much she actually did appreciate that Noah had been there, especially when she realized how much worse the situation would likely have become without him.

She looked deeper into his dark eyes and said, "I really did appreciate it."

His smile went slightly lopsided, as if she were embarrassing him, and he said, "I'm glad to help."

He reached out and took her by the arms then, a

friendly, supportive gesture, as if to only let her know he genuinely was there for her. But the minute those strong, callused hands came into contact with her bare skin, that contact became something more significant.

Marti felt it. She knew Noah did, too, because his grip tightened just enough to add a hint of intimacy and his thumbs began a little massaging motion.

She also saw in his expression that gears had been switched.

He was thinking about kissing her—she knew it as surely as she knew she was thinking about having him kiss her.

But would he do it?

She wanted him to. She didn't understand it, and she again felt guilty and disloyal for it. But somewhere inside her head there was a voice saying: *Kiss me... Kiss me...*

Then he did.

But it was so not what she'd had in mind.

He pulled her toward him and he pressed his warm, soft mouth to her forehead.

Her forehead, not her lips!

She swallowed hard but this time it wasn't to keep her dinner down, it was to keep something else entirely at bay—the urge to tip her chin and kiss him for real as he lingered there, the scent of a clean, woodsy cologne just making her want him to kiss her all the more.

But that wasn't what was going on between them now, she reminded herself. This wasn't Denver. They weren't drunk. They couldn't claim to be carried away by the moment. This was the real world, they were in an awkward predicament working hard to just get acquainted.

She swallowed again and drew back, though not enough to pull away, only enough to tilt her head and look up at him again, from a much closer vantage point.

But still Noah didn't take the hint. He drew back, too, let go of her arms and took a step away from her.

"Tomorrow," he said, as if even that kiss hadn't happened. Or wasn't important enough to comment on.

"I'll see you tomorrow," she parroted, fighting to keep her voice level and free of the disappointment that was running through her.

Then Noah turned around and went back to his truck, and Marti went inside, closed the door and wilted against it.

What *was* it about that man?

He wasn't Jack. He wasn't anything like Jack. Noah was tall where Jack had barely been five-ten. Noah was laid-back where Jack had been like an energetic, over-grown kid. Noah was dark where Jack had been blond and blue-eyed. Noah worked quietly and methodically with his hands where Jack had been a fast-talking, hit-it-with-everything-he-had salesman. The two men were polar opposites.

And yet that didn't seem to matter because something about Noah just kept pulling her toward him in spite of herself and the feelings she still had for Jack. In spite of grief and good sense. In spite of the fact that she hardly knew Noah. And she didn't know what to do about it.

It seemed as if she should fight it.

Shouldn't she?

Or should she just go with the flow since she was already carrying Noah's baby?

She honestly didn't know. It was all just so confusing.

And it didn't help when one other thing occurred to her as she pushed away from the door and headed up the steps to her bedroom.

She'd thought that alcohol had played the biggest role in that night in Denver. But here she was now, wishing that she was still out on the porch with Noah.

That he was taking her into his arms, holding her close, kissing her until her lips were raw.

And unless she was mistaken, she wanted it even more now than she had at any point that night in Denver.

Only now she was perfectly sober.

And under the influence of nothing but the man himself.

Chapter Six

"Betty next door told me at church on Sunday that she's retirin' and closin' the quilt shop so that'll free up all four of my places. I'm lookin' to sell out the whole lot of 'em. I'm ready to retire, too, sit on my porch and play with my grandkids," Arnie Newman said in response to Marti's concerns that the three adjoining storefronts she and Noah were looking at on Wednesday afternoon weren't enough space for the Northbridge Home-Max.

"What about weight-bearing walls?" Noah asked. "You said originally these four stores were two—you split them up yourself. So which separating walls can just be removed and which will have to be cut into and re-braced?"

Marti told herself to listen to the answer, to try to concentrate on that and keep her mind off of Noah.

But they'd come straight from his day's work in her grandmother's house and the man even managed to look sexy in grubby jeans and an almost threadbare chambray shirt. Plus there was a little sawdust in his hair that she was dying to brush out just so she could see if his hair was as soft as she thought she remembered. And, as with the entire night before and the rest of this day, the notion of him kissing her just kept haunting her.

He's talking to you...

She yanked herself out of those other thoughts she'd drifted into when Noah began saying something to her about breaking through separating walls and using reinforced columns as support.

"Is that a job you could do?" she asked.

"Sure," Noah said.

"You can trust 'im, too," Arnie Newman contributed. "Time was, we all thought this one was no good. But he came out of it and now there's nobody in town wouldn't hand over the keys to their house and trust 'im to do the best work you could get done anywheres. He's built whole houses from the ground up around here and done a job to be proud of."

Arnie had turned to speak directly to Marti, and from behind him Noah made a face at what the older man was saying. Marti knew he appreciated the endorsement but the praise seemed to embarrass him.

Or was it the backhanded way the endorsement had begun that made him uncomfortable?

Reining in her wandering thoughts a second time, she said, "I'll have to talk it over with my brothers, but the fourth storefront would give us enough square footage, the location is great and if Noah can do the construction, I don't see any reason why this wouldn't be a perfect place for Home-Max."

"And don't worry about Hector Tyson swooping this one out from under you," Arnie said—apparently Tyson's deal had somehow become common knowledge already. "I wouldn't sell that buzzard three quarters for a dollar."

"I appreciate that," Marti said.

"I gotta get goin', though," Arnie added in a sudden hurry. "I'll leave you two here to look over anything else you might want to. Just lock up when you're done, Noah." Then, pretending that he was confiding in her, the older man said, "Like I told you, I can trust 'im now and so can you."

"Good to know," Marti said before they all exchanged parting amenities and Arnie left.

"Umm…are you a reformed criminal or something? Should I be worried for my safety?" she asked Noah to goad him when they were alone, not really believing he had anything too notorious in his past or that she was in any danger from him.

Noah shook his head and rolled his eyes. "You have to be careful what you do in a small town—you never live it down."

Marti had been checking out the heating vents in the floor and ended up near the stairs that led to the upper level. She stopped there to turn and look at Noah. He was standing in the center of the vacant store and she couldn't help appreciating the sight of him with his hands hooked nonchalantly in his pockets, his weight slung more on one hip than the other.

"What did you do that you can't live down?" she asked.

He shrugged. "Adolescence came in with a bang. And pretty much went out with one, too," he answered, that last part sounding like a double entendre but Marti didn't understand why.

"You're still trying to live down *puberty*?" she said with a laugh.

"I was a rebellious kid."

"Really?" Somehow Marti hadn't pictured him that way. "How *rebellious* were you?"

"Well, two of the three other guys in the group I hung out with are in jail now…"

"Seriously?"

"They robbed a gas station in Billings last year."

"Oh," Marti said, starting to wonder if he actually did have a notorious past. "Did you do things like that?"

"Not *that* bad. But there was some unlawful activity."

"What kind of unlawful activity?" Marti asked, still finding it hard to believe of him.

"Things like mailbox bashing. We'd hang out the window of a car and see how many we could hit out of the park with a baseball bat as we drove by. Arnie's mailbox was one of those and I was the hitter that night— it went flying through his living-room window. He was sitting in a chair right under the window, the mailbox grazed his bald head, the glass cut him up pretty good and he had to go to the emergency room for stitches."

"That *is* kind of a big deal," Marti said.

"Yeah," Noah agreed. "We'd gotten away with vandalizing the mailboxes up to then because we'd been sneaking out about two in the morning to do it. But that night Arnie had fallen asleep in his chair and his wife had just come out to wake him up and make him go to bed when I hit their mailbox. She saw me. If Northbridge wasn't a small town I would have been in for vandalism and assault charges, but Arnie didn't want that and everybody else whose mailboxes we'd bashed gave us a break, too. We had to replace all the mailboxes and my family made me work at the Newman place doing chores for six months to pay off the window and Arnie's medical bills, but we didn't end up with a criminal record."

"Was that the extent of your lawbreaking?" Marti asked, sensing that it wasn't.

"There was some shoplifting—candy, gum, small things, but still, we stole them. There was some underage drinking and driving—yes, at the same time—and I was the one drunk and driving when we got pulled over. That kept me from getting my driver's license until I was eighteen. There was graffiti on the side of a barn—again, my doing—so I had to spend the summer repainting it to make up for that." He was clearly not proud of any of it and didn't want to continue talking about himself even though she was reasonably sure he hadn't told her everything.

"Sounds like a little more than basic teenage rebellion," Marti pointed out.

"It may sound like it, but that was all it was. Don't forget, I was the Reverend's grandson. His fire-and-brimstone sermons at church every Sunday were nothing compared to what we had to listen to at home over dinner. We couldn't just be good, we had to be *better* than everyone. We had to set the highest example—"

"And instead you decided to set the lowest?" Marti joked gently.

"Yeah, to be honest, that was what I decided to do—in my not-so-rational, definitely not-reasonable teenage brain. I went looking for trouble just to prove the Reverend couldn't tell me what and who I had to be. I'd watched my father and my uncle bend to his will on everything and I wasn't going to do it, too. I was going to show him and anybody else who was watching that the Reverend was not in control of me."

"Wow. Is that what I'm in for when this baby hits puberty?"

Noah's expression had been somber but he cracked a smile at that. "Hopefully not. But there were a lot of warnings about payback from my own kids."

"Oh, good," Marti said facetiously.

Noah crossed to her on long strides with a hint of natural swagger to his walk and stopped close in front of her.

"I never blew anything up," he challenged, referring to her cherry bomb in the fridge story of the previous evening.

He was so close. He was directly in front of her. He was looking down into her eyes. How could she *not* think about him kissing her?

Still, she tried. Even as she angled her chin upward. "I don't have friends in prison," she countered.

Noah laughed. "Neither do I—just *former* friends. The two in jail are brothers and we parted ways when they moved to Billings. Once they were gone I discovered girls were more fun."

He was standing near enough that when he spoke she caught a whiff of clean, minty breath that only made thoughts of kissing all the stronger. And how could he still smell good even after working all day?

Marti's chin rose another fraction of an inch. "Is the discovery that girls were more fun how your adolescence went out with a bang?" she asked with the same double entendre he'd used before.

But something about that sobered him again. "Let's just say things happened and I finally opted to clean up my act."

"You aren't going to tell me what *things* happened?"

He seemed to reconsider. But then he shook his head again and spun away from her on his boot heels. "Always leave 'em wanting more, it brings 'em back," he joked. "Besides, you wanted to take another look upstairs to see about putting the offices there, didn't you?"

So he had a bit of a stubborn streak. That was the first Marti had seen of it. A stubborn streak and a strong will. He'd been so accommodating until then that it surprised her. And yet it didn't make him less appealing, it made him all the more appealing. Or maybe she was just particularly hormonal today…

But she didn't pursue the subject of his checkered past as they climbed the steps to the upper floor because he'd just told her to what lengths he would go in the opposite direction when someone pressured him. Besides, she hadn't been forthcoming about her own history yet so she didn't think she had any basis for pushing.

Plus she had something else she wanted to talk to him about and after counting electrical outlets on the second floor, with Noah assuring her he could add as many as she needed, Marti stopped to look through one of the windows, then turned her back to it and leaned her hips against the sill.

"Speaking of your grandfather…" she said.

"I thought we were speaking of adding a bigger breaker box to accommodate rewiring up here," Noah said from where he was hunkered down checking an outlet.

"We were, but you said you could do that and I didn't think there was any more to say about it. Is there?"

"No," he admitted, standing again.

He headed for her once more and she decided that his biggest crime was how those jeans rode his narrow hips. It took all she could muster to keep from staring. And drooling.

When he got to her, he leaned a shoulder against the edge of the window and Marti turned a hip into the sill to sit facing him.

"Okay, speaking of my grandfather," he allowed then.

"I talked to my grandmother about Hector Tyson today."

"Now that's something we can sink our teeth into."

So he'd thought she was trying to get back to talking about his past.

"Is that why Theresa was upset when I came into the sunroom?" he asked.

"Yes. And by the way, thanks for getting her out of it. Usually only Ry can distract her like that when something sets her off."

Noah had teased her grandmother a little, cajoled her a little, flattered her a little, and it had all worked to keep Theresa from hysterics.

"Sure," Noah said in acceptance of her gratitude, as if it had been nothing when, in fact, Marti had not only appreciated it, she'd been impressed by it, too.

But she knew that saying more about it would only embarrass him the way Arnie Newman's praise had, so she merely continued.

"Before I talked to Gram, I talked to my brother Ry. He met with our lawyers and they think we have grounds to sue Tyson since Gram was underage and under duress when she sold him the land. They think he owes her restitution—by not giving her an even remotely fair price for the land, he basically swindled her. He'll be served an intent-to-sue notice as soon as it's drawn up—in the next day or two."

"He won't like that," Noah said matter-of-factly.

"No, I'm sure he won't. But when I told Gram that's what we were doing—that it was the best that could be done since the land and the houses on it belong to so many other people now, she couldn't have cared less. She did something similar to this with Wyatt, too, a few weeks ago—she said Tyson had taken something more important than land from her. Wyatt couldn't get her to tell him what she was talking about and I tried pressing her again today."

"Did she tell you?"

"All I could get out of her was that it wasn't about the land and that Hector told her she couldn't tell anyone. But she also said that the minister and the minister's wife told her the same thing—that's the first any of us have heard about her taking her problems to a minister. Gram said the minister told her she had to do what was right even if it wasn't what was right for her. I was wondering if the minister she was talking about is your grandfather and if he might be able to shed some light on this."

Noah shook his handsome head again. "My grandfather is not a helpful guy. But you're in luck—he wouldn't be the minister your grandmother is talking about. If I'm up to date on the grapevine, Theresa left here in 1950, right?"

"Right."

"Well, my grandparents didn't move to Northbridge until just after that."

"Really? For some reason I thought you were all natives."

"Nope. My grandparents came here to take over when the previous minister died unexpectedly of a heart attack—that would be the minister who was here when Theresa was."

"So how am I in luck if he died decades ago?"

"Because that minister's wife is still alive and well and living right here in town. I just did some work for her a few months ago. And didn't you say the minister's wife told your grandmother something? She must have been in on whatever it was Theresa went to talk about."

Pleased with that news, Marti smiled up at him. "Will you make up for keeping part of your misspent youth a secret by taking me to meet the former minister's wife?"

Noah returned her smile with a wry one of his own. "I'm not keeping it a *secret* from you. I'm just not sure this is the right time to tell you about it. It's a tough subject for me. I wouldn't want you getting any wrong ideas about me."

"A mystery wrapped in a riddle—what could you possibly tell me about your teenage years that could give me bad ideas?"

He didn't respond to that with anything but raised eyebrows.

"Curiosity killed the cat, you know. It can't be good for pregnant women," Marti said then.

He smiled bigger and shook his head as if he were enjoying this.

Then, completely without warning, he swooped in and kissed her on the lips. But so quickly she didn't even have the chance to pucker up and kiss him back. Or feel as if she'd actually *been* kissed. Again.

"What was that for?" she asked, wondering if she could get him to do a replay.

"I just felt like it."

"It's not going to make me any less curious, if that's what you think," she warned.

Noah laughed. "I'll tell you what, some of us local guys have a sports team called the Bruisers. We play whatever is in season and tonight is the last basketball game. Come to that, come with me to Adz afterward for the last-game celebration—that's our local pub. And maybe—maybe—we can talk about me and my dark part some more."

"I can't tonight—I felt guilty for upsetting Gram today and promised her a game-night tonight—board games, not basketball."

"Okay," he renegotiated, "skip my game to spend that time with your grandmother, meet me at Adz afterward. If you want to hear about my lost years—"

Marti laughed. "There were lost years?"

"No, I just thought it sounded good. But if you want to hear about what got me out of being a badass kid, the only chance you have is if you show up at Adz tonight."

Marti pretended to think it over. And it *was* only pretense because she already knew she was going to the pub tonight, not only to have her curiosity satisfied, but to see Noah again.

She wasn't going to let him know that, though. So she stood and said, "I'll think about it."

Then she did what she'd been wanting to do since

they'd left the house—she reached up and brushed the sawdust out of his hair, finding that it *was* every bit as soft as she'd recalled. And even that small amount of contact was enough to ignite something in the air between them.

Which was when Noah leaned forward and kissed her a second time.

Shocked yet again, at least he stayed long enough for the kiss to register. But just barely. Warm, supple lips touched hers and then were gone again a split second later—that was all she knew.

Still, it was enough to leave her wanting more.

But she wasn't going to let him know *that*, either.

"Just because you felt like it?" she asked, repeating his earlier words but not expecting her voice to come out so breathy and quiet and affected by that brief kiss.

"'Fraid so," he answered. "Is that bad?"

"I've had better," she goaded him, clearly referring to the kiss itself rather than to whether or not he should have kissed her.

The goad just made him chuckle as if he knew something she didn't know on that score, too. But all he said was, "I'll try harder next time. Tonight, maybe…"

Marti laughed at his cockiness. "I'm playing board games with my grandmother tonight," she countered as if there was still a chance she wouldn't show up at Adz after his game.

"We'll see," Noah said as they headed for the stairs.

And as they each got into their vehicles outside,

Marti was once more bouncing from feelings of disloy-
alty and guilt to eagerness to see Noah again later.

And maybe to also get a taste of what it was like
when he tried harder.

Chapter Seven

"Man, you were on fire tonight!" Ad Walker said to Noah, handing him the beer that kicked off the last-basketball-game-of-the-season party Wednesday evening.

Noah merely smiled at the comment and the pat on the back he received from the owner of Adz, the popular local hangout.

Noah *had* had a good game, but he thought there was another reason for the fire in him tonight. And her name was Marti Grayson.

Taking the single beer he was in the mood for tonight, Noah made his way through the crowded establishment to reach the prime spot for watching the door. He'd already checked out the whole place to make sure Marti hadn't arrived ahead of him, and since she hadn't, he wanted to be able to see her the minute she came in.

If she came.

He thought she'd just been giving him a hard time this afternoon by not committing to tonight, but he didn't know her well enough to be sure. Still, his hopes were high as he propped himself on a barstool in the corner nearest the dartboard and took a drink of his beer.

The door opened then and his hopes got even higher. Only to deflate a moment later when the wives of three of his teammates filed through and still there was no Marti.

Damn.

What if she didn't come? Maybe he should call her. Maybe he should go to the house. Maybe he should just accept that she might blow tonight off and be cool about it…

He didn't know. Hell, he didn't know what he was doing all the way around when it came to Marti.

He was *supposed* to be just getting to know her. He was *supposed* to be just letting her get to know him. But he was having a tough time leaving it at that. He'd been attracted to Marti in Denver and that attraction was springing back to life with a vengeance. What was he supposed to do about *that?* Give in to it or fight it?

Under other circumstances being attracted to the mother of his child wouldn't have a downside. But under these circumstances he wasn't so sure. Under these circumstances it seemed that a calm, rational handling of everything, a friendly but middle-of-the-road connection, was the safest way for him to go.

The trouble was, he wasn't doing so well at reining in his attraction to Marti, and there was nothing calm or rational or middle-of-the-road about it. The attraction was stronger willed than Dilly. And like his donkey, it had a mind of its own. Which was why kissing had come into the picture last night and again this afternoon.

And maybe because of the kissing, Marti wasn't showing up now, he thought. Maybe the thought that he might kiss her again tonight was keeping her away. Maybe she wasn't attracted to him. Or maybe a connection with him just wasn't what she wanted and if he pushed her, if he made her uncomfortable, she wouldn't want anything to do with him. And that could get him cut off from the baby...

He took a long drink of his beer and tried to get a grip on himself.

He had to be careful about what he was doing when it came to Marti and the baby. He knew it. He tried not to lose sight of that. It was just that every minute he was with Marti, every glimpse of her as he worked at her grandmother's house, every sound of her voice, made it worse for him. And if there wasn't a baby and the risk of that baby being kept from him, nothing would be holding him back.

But there *was* a baby and that meant that he couldn't just let his attraction run rampant. He had to make sure he didn't somehow alienate her.

So if she didn't show up tonight he wasn't calling, he

told himself. He wasn't going by her house. He wouldn't say a word about it when he saw her at work tomorrow.

But come on, show up…

More people filed into the restaurant and each time the door opened, his high hopes got a little lower.

Had those stupid little kisses put her off? He hadn't thought so at the time.

She'd seemed surprised by them—hell, *he'd* been surprised by them. They certainly hadn't been planned. He simply hadn't been able to resist the urge that had come with looking into her beautiful face. With wanting to touch that silky, sun-kissed hair. With catching that sparkle of mischief in those silver-blue eyes.

She hadn't balked, though. Or gotten mad at him. She'd just teased him about the kisses not being great— that didn't seem like he'd done any harm. It seemed as if it had just brought out more of the mischief in her.

Which he'd liked. He liked that she could hold her own, give as good as she got, that she wasn't the kind of woman who pretended to be whatever she thought someone wanted her to be.

Who was he kidding? He liked everything about her. And yes, that meant he *wanted* to kiss her again, and if she walked through that door right now and he got to spend the next few hours with her, he couldn't say he *wouldn't* kiss her again…

So what was he going to do?

He drank more beer.

And then he made his decision.

If Marti showed up tonight, in spite of this desire

for her, he'd take it as a sign that he hadn't already alienated her.

But if she didn't show, he'd take that as a sign that he'd better find a way to control himself and keep things between them calm and rational and middle-of-the-road. He'd better find a way never to kiss her again. To just be friends.

He took another slug of beer and trained his eyes on that door, willing it to open, willing Marti to walk through it.

Then the door did open again.

Someone moved into his line of vision and blocked his view. He craned his neck to see around them, feeling slightly frantic.

The door closed before he could see who had come in so he did a quick scan of everyone anywhere near the entrance.

And that was when he got his sign.

Standing in the midst of his friends and neighbors and family was Marti.

Marti didn't understand why, but when she spotted Noah it was as if every other person in the place faded into a blur and all she could see clearly was him.

He looked gorgeous, as usual. Low-slung jeans. A white T-shirt with short sleeves stretched tight over bulging biceps. His hair was freshly washed and carelessly combed. His jaw was clean shaven. There was a wide smile on that face that packed a wallop and set her stomach fluttering.

"You made it," he said when he reached her side, sounding more pleased than she'd expected.

"After taking a bad beating at Scrabble I needed a breather," she responded, shouting to be heard over the noise in the place.

"Let's go somewhere quieter and get you something to drink," Noah suggested, wrapping a protective arm around her shoulders to help her weave through tables and all of the people sitting and standing at them.

His arm around her was nothing, Marti told herself. Nothing more than anyone might do in a place that full. But somehow she was ultra-aware of every point of contact—of his hand on her left arm where the short sleeve of her own T-shirt stopped, and her bare skin drank in the feel of his callused palm and long fingers; of his strong arm pressed across her back, of her right shoulder tucked so perfectly into his side.

It's nothing…

And yet it was enough to send more than her stomach twittering. Enough for her to be barely aware of the ac-colades for Noah's basketball playing that followed them, barely aware of anything but him.

He guided her into an adjoining room with a pool table at its center and a few small booths outlining the walls. While this room was hardly unoccupied—there was a game going on and a group gathered around to watch—it wasn't as crowded, and that removed the need for Noah's arm around her. So he let go. And Marti felt distinct and unmistakable disappointment when he did.

She only hoped it didn't show.

Noah pointed to a tiny corner booth that was the only one free. "We'll have to sit on top of each other but at least we can sit," he said.

He waited for Marti to precede him to the corner and slide in before he slid in with her. And while they didn't have to literally sit on top of each other, they did end up so near that his thigh ran the length of hers—something not quite as titillating as his arm around her, but close.

A waitress appeared almost instantly, showering Noah with more praise for the game Marti hadn't seen, then taking Marti's order of a lemonade.

When the waitress left, Noah stretched an arm along the back of the booth and although it wasn't exactly touching her, between the feel of having it nearby and the press of his thigh to hers under the table, that twittering sensation began all over again.

Nervous excitement—that's all it was, Marti told herself. It didn't have anything to do with being so near to him that she was almost cocooned by his big body, or the fact that she was still thinking about those kisses this afternoon, or his playful threat of more to come…

"I was beginning to wonder if you were going to stand me up tonight," Noah said then.

"Worried?" she joked.

"I was," he said as if he hadn't been at all.

The waitress returned with Marti's drink. Marti waited for the woman to leave again and then said, "I think if I hadn't come tonight you could probably have still found some company." She nodded in the direction of the waitress who was smiling flirtatiously at Noah as she headed to another table.

Noah barely spared the other woman a glance before resettling his gaze on Marti and smiling audaciously. "Does that mean I'm going home with you tonight?"

Marti laughed but didn't take the bait. "Nice try," she said. Then she changed the subject because it was bad enough to be constantly thinking about Noah kissing her, she didn't need to add the idea of taking him home. "So, your game went well tonight?" she asked.

Noah shrugged as if it were no big deal. "I was the high scorer. I'm sure it couldn't compare to playing Scrabble with Theresa and Mary Pat, though," he teased.

"Well, no, but then what could?" Marti countered after tasting her lemonade. Then she said, "Funny, but I didn't hear anything about you being on the high school basketball team in that story you told me today about your misspent youth. You wouldn't have been making some of that up, would you? When the truth is you were really just a quiet, unassuming jock who had a mishap or two like every kid does?"

Noah grinned, looked away from her and called to a man talking to a group at another table. "Hey, Ad! You ever play basketball—or any other sport with me—in high school?"

"Are you having a blackout or something? The only thing you did with a basketball in high school was put it through a window in the gym. You spent a month in detention for that. Wasn't that your extracurricular activity—detention?"

Everyone laughed, including Noah who then looked back at Marti with an I-told-you-so expression. "Need to hear more?"

"Okay, so you really were a badass. And if that's the case then part of why I came here tonight was to hear what finally happened to make you clean up your act."

He was in no hurry to answer her. She watched him take a drink of the beer he was slowly nursing, oddly aware of his hand around the bottle, of the flex of the muscles of his forearm as he gripped it, the tendons in his sculpted jaw as his head tipped back, of his lips pressed to the mouth of the bottleneck...

What was going on with her tonight? She sipped her own beverage in an attempt to refocus.

Then, thinking that she was going to win this tug-of-war with him if it was the last thing she did, she said, "Let's have it, Perry, or I'm out of here."

But still he stalled, taking yet another swig of beer, and Marti had the distinct impression that he really didn't want to talk about this.

She merely waited.

Then, with his eyes on the beer bottle and his thumb fiddling with a loose edge of the label, he said, "I told you there was a point where I discovered that girls were more fun than wreaking havoc. Well, there was one girl in particular. Sandy Huff." He paused again, clearly not eager to go on. But he shrugged and sighed and did anyway. "I got her pregnant when she was sixteen and I was seventeen."

Marti had not seen that one coming and she didn't know what to say.

Luckily Noah continued without any encouragement. "I know what you're thinking—doesn't this guy ever learn? But believe it or not—and unlike our drunken omission of a condom—I was using protection with Sandy. It just wasn't foolproof and we were in trouble. I thought we should get married—"

"At sixteen and seventeen?"

"Teenage hormones and my big-man bravado and first love and then a baby? Sure, getting married seemed like exactly what we should do. It seemed like the *right* thing to do. So we got our parents together and I laid out the whole package—she was pregnant, we wanted to get married and keep the baby."

"How did that go over?"

"My parents were just sort of shell-shocked. On top of everything else they'd had to deal with from me they just looked beaten. But Sandy's parents went berserk."

Marti nodded, recalling her own panic at this pregnancy she was just now becoming accustomed to.

"Sandy's father had hated me from the start and forbidden her to hang out with me," Noah went on. "So I was the no-good troublemaker his daughter had been sneaking behind his back to see. There was no way he was going for the marriage scenario."

"So you decided to straighten yourself out to make you more worthy of his daughter?" Marti guessed.

Noah's half smile was wry and humorless. "I wish I'd been that smart. No, actually, I played tough guy—

I shot off my mouth, put a hole in the wall with my fist, basically proved her father right in believing I was no good. We were at Sandy's house and her father kicked me and my family out, and threatened to shoot me on sight if I ever went near his daughter again."

"What did you do?"

"I got to her through her best friend and tried to convince her to run away with me."

It was still difficult to believe that the man sitting beside her had begun as the boy he was describing, but Marti could also see how fiercely this had all affected him, how much he hated that that was the kid he'd been, and her heart went out to him.

"Did you run away?" she asked.

Noah shook his head. "Sandy started backing off. She was a scared kid, I was a hothead—I think my response to her father just freaked her out even more. I know it pushed her in the direction of her parents' opinion about how things should go from there."

He paused and Marti had the impression he would have rather eaten nails than finish. But then he did anyway—in a voice that was quiet, defensive and full of regret.

"She ended up having an abortion."

When he said that, his head tilted, his chin went up slightly with it and it was almost a flinch. And between that and the tone in which he'd confessed that last part, Marti thought that he needed a moment before she said, "Is that what you were afraid might influence me?"

Noah shrugged with his eyebrows and finally looked

from the beer bottle to her. "It was like a mule kick to me seventeen years ago. I didn't want to plant any ideas—"

"I already told you—"

"I know, but it happened to me once and—"

"How did an abortion happen to *you?*"

"Yeah, that probably does sound weird, doesn't it? But here's the thing—it was still my baby. Not my body, but still my baby. Maybe that sounds crazy to you or seems like it shouldn't matter—especially to a contrary seventeen-year-old kid. But the baby was real to me. And when Sandy's parents talked her into having an abortion a big part of their argument was based on what a screwup I was. On what a mistake it would be all the way around to have *my* baby."

He paused, and Marti could see just how strong an impact that had had on him.

"Of all the trouble I'd been in," he said, "of all the consequences of my actions up to then, nothing had hit me as hard as the thought that if I *had* been the quiet, unassuming jock who everyone liked, our parents might have been more on our side. And even if the whole marriage idea hadn't played out, at least we might have been able to have the baby and make that work out somehow. And after that, proving that my grandfather didn't have a hold over me, showing him I could do whatever I wanted, just didn't seem as important as being someone whose kids were worth bringing into the world."

Marti honestly didn't know what to say to that and was actually glad when just then Noah's name was called from the main room and demands were shouted for him to join his teammates.

"Don't make us drag you in here!" came one threat that left no choice.

"Sorry. Looks like we're not going to be left to our corner," Noah said, but Marti thought he was just as glad to escape their conversation.

"I guess it's the price to be paid for being here with the star player," she teased him as he slid out of the booth and waited for her to go with him.

Marti spent the rest of the evening by Noah's side as he was teased and toasted, as the highlights of his game were relived. By all accounts he'd played better than anyone had ever seen anyone play in one of the local games. What impressed Marti was how humble Noah was in response to it all.

He tried several times to put an end to the accolades, to make a getaway for them, but his friends wouldn't have it and not until the place was finally closing did the celebration disband.

Outside of Adz there was a succession of more pats on the back for Noah, then everyone went in separate directions and Marti had Noah's undivided attention again— too late to do more with it than let him walk her to her car.

"I talked to Emmalina," he said along the way.

"Emmalina?"

"Emmalina Dewell—the wife of the minister who your grandmother would have gone to see when she was a girl. She said she'd be happy to talk to us tomorrow night at seven. Will that work?"

"You already arranged for that? You're fast," Marti marveled.

"It's a small town, it doesn't take a lot to get people together. So what do you say?" he asked as they passed the Groceries and Sundries and arrived at her brother's SUV. "I thought we might be able to grab a bite to eat afterward?"

"Sure. Okay," Marti agreed, looking forward to spending some more time with Noah, one-on-one.

She unlocked the car door but before she could open it, he maneuvered himself between her and the SUV, leaning back against it so she couldn't open the door.

"You aren't ready to run for the hills, are you?"

That confused her.

"Run for the hills?" she repeated.

"Did I scare you off by telling you I was basically a thug as a kid?"

Marti couldn't help smiling. "You're not still a thug, are you? Or have I just overlooked it?"

"Hand to God, I am not," he swore, actually holding up his hand.

"Then no, I won't run for the hills."

"Good," he said. "Because I'm a good guy."

Marti laughed. "Yeah, I think you just might be."

"Do you? Is that why you came tonight or was it only to get the full picture of just how rotten I was?"

Marti could hear in Noah's voice, see in his expression that it was important to him to know. And while she felt as if she were exposing herself, she opted not to joke or give him a hard time.

"I came because I *do* think you're a good guy."

It was hardly kudos or a declaration of undying love but it made him flash a cocky and very sexy grin. "And you like me," he added himself.

"Oh, now you're pushing it," she said. But he'd made her smile, too, so the chastisement was hardly believable.

"It's just a beginning," he said as if he were trying to keep her from shying away. "I'm happy to know you can stand me, is all."

"Barely," she said airily because she'd already shown him enough.

He was undaunted, though, still grinning down at her. "I like you, too," he confided. "And if you weren't pregnant…"

And then the joking stopped. Something different heated the air between them. In the glow of the street lights she saw Noah's eyes soften, and there was something else reflected in his handsome face—something that didn't make her feel at all like an untouchable pregnant woman, something that made her feel the way she had when Jack was focused intently—and appreciatively—on her.

But this was Noah and she was very, very aware of that.

And somehow okay with it…

Then, in a deep, intimate voice, Noah said, "Thanks for coming tonight."

"I'm sorry I missed your game."

"Doesn't matter. I'm just glad you came to Adz afterward."

"Me, too," she admitted in a hushed voice.

For a moment he merely went on looking at her, into her eyes. Then he raised a hand to the side of her face, his palm following the curve of her jaw to hold it, to tip it enough so that his mouth could meet hers.

There was a moment of déjà vu for Marti—not exactly a memory of that night they'd spent together but a sense of familiarity.

Noah deepened the kiss. His breath was warm against her skin and sweet with the mint he'd had after his beer. His hand was strong and gentle, his touch drawing her to him, holding her there, making it impossible to be aware of anything but Noah.

And even though this kiss lasted long enough for every detail to register, to brand itself on her brain as Noah's kiss and only Noah's kiss, it still ended much, much too soon.

Now there was cool evening air where there had been the heat of him and she opened her eyes to find his lids slowly rising, too.

"Better?" he asked, harking back to her remark that afternoon that she'd had kisses that were better than those little pecks he'd given earlier.

"Better. And I couldn't even tell you were trying harder," she goaded, also referencing what had been said before.

"Smooth as ice—that's me," he countered with a satisfied smile before he kissed her again—shorter, lighter, more playfully and certainly not picking up where he'd left off. Unfortunately...

He slipped out from between her and the car and

opened the door for her. And since she couldn't very well ignore it, she got behind the wheel.

"I have some materials to pick up tomorrow and a bid to work on for the Home-Max that those new people are opening up," he said, teasing her. "So I won't be at your grandmother's house during the day. I'll just come by and get you about a quarter to seven to go to Emmalina's."

Marti nodded. "I'll be ready," she said as she started the engine.

They exchanged good-nights and Noah closed the door, leaving Marti to back away from the curb. He waved as she put the car in gear and she returned the wave before heading down Main toward South Street, looking for him again in her rearview mirror, finding him still there, watching her go.

She thought back to that first flashback to their night in Denver. How she'd wondered if she'd liked the way Noah kissed as much as she'd liked the way Jack had.

And now she knew.

They didn't kiss anything alike. They were as distinctly different at that as they were in everything else.

But she had been right—she liked Noah's kiss as much as she'd liked Jack's. Noah Perry definitely had a power all his own.

And she was feeling the impact.

Chapter Eight

"So where does Emmalina Dewell live?" Marti asked on Thursday evening as they drove to see the former minister's wife.

Noah kept his eyes on the road as he answered. "Emmalina is eighty-nine now. She has a small house on the very edge of town, right next door to her daughter's house. Lila keeps an eye on her, but Emmalina does all right for herself."

"Is Lila her only child?"

"Nooo, Lila and three others are the kids Emmalina had with her first husband—the minister. A year after he died, Emmalina married Harvey Forester and had two more kids. She married at least two more times over the next thirty years or so."

"So after all that, do you think she'll remember as far back as my grandmother?"

"I wouldn't be wasting your time if I didn't think so. Emmalina is as sharp as you or I. And when I called her and told her you were Theresa Hobbs's granddaughter, that you wanted to talk about Theresa from before she left Northbridge, Emmalina didn't even need reminding who Theresa might be. Of course there's been a lot of talk about Theresa since she showed up in Northbridge, so I'm sure my call wasn't the first Emmalina has heard about Theresa being back. But yeah, I trust her memory."

He made a U-turn then and parked at the curb in front of the second to the last house on South Street, before open road and cornfields marked the beginning of the farm- and ranchland that also made up Northbridge. The house was no bigger than a double garage, painted bright pink with white trim.

Noah must have seen Marti's shock at the color because he laughed. "Yep, this is Emmalina's place," he said as he got out of the truck and came around to the curbside to open Marti's door. "But don't let the color of her house or the number of husbands she's had fool you. Emmalina is a little old grandma through and through."

Marti wasn't sure what that meant but she stepped out onto the sidewalk in front of the pristine white picket fence that surrounded the front yard of the flamboyantly painted residence anyway.

Noah opened the gate and waited for Marti to go

ahead of him, closing the gate behind them once they were both within the perimeter. Then they went side by side up onto the porch.

The front door was open so he knocked on the frame of the screen door and called, "Emmalina? It's Noah."

"Come in, sweetheart! Come in! I'm in the kitchen," a lilting voice called back.

Noah opened the screen door for Marti and she entered a tiny living room decorated in dated furniture that didn't at all reflect the bold color choice on the outside of the house. He led Marti to the tiny kitchen.

"What do I smell?" he asked, smiling.

"You know..." was the answer from the woman who turned to them when they joined her.

Emmalina was tiny. At least three inches under five feet tall, she was roly-poly, her well-lined face was made-up with slightly too much blush, her white hair was styled like a cotton-candy bubble around her head and she was dressed in sky blue knit pants and a flowered blouse of the same hue, with an apron protecting the front of her.

"Tamales!" Noah said when she held up a platter of them to show him what was causing the delicious aroma they'd walked into. Then to Marti he said, "Emmalina's homemade tamales are straight from heaven."

"And all for you today, for coming to see me."

Noah bent over and kissed the chubby cheek of the elderly woman.

Then he said, "This is Marti Grayson, Emmalina, Theresa's granddaughter."

"Oh, so pretty! Make this one share his tamales with you."

"I will," Marti assured her with a laugh.

"Let's you and me sit while I wrap them up," Emmalina suggested to Marti, motioning to the small kitchen table pushed against one wall. "But you, Noah, I need a favor from."

"Anything."

"My big spoon fell behind the stove yesterday. Can you move it out and get it for me?"

"I think I can do that," he said.

Emmalina went to the kitchen table and set the platter of tamales there, pulling out a vinyl chair for Marti to sit on one side of the table with her back to the wall, while Emmalina sat just around the corner with her back to Noah, meticulously wrapping each tamale in foil.

It made it impossible for Marti to look at Emmalina without Noah also being in her line of vision.

He was dressed in jeans and a red polo shirt that accentuated his broad shoulders and muscular arms. Marti had been aware of every detail since the minute she'd opened the door to greet him tonight, but when all of those well-toned muscles began to flex to work the heavy stove away from the facing wall, she couldn't tear her gaze away.

Oh, what this guy did to her! She couldn't keep from thinking about him. And since he'd kissed her again, she hadn't been able to stop reliving it and daydreaming about it. And now the mere sight of him doing something as simple as moving a stove was making her temperature rise about twenty degrees. Forget about concentrating on anything else—she just couldn't do it...

Finally he finished and joined them at the table. As he pulled his chair over it occurred to Marti that this kind of...obsession, she supposed, had never happened with Jack.

Certainly she'd thought he was great-looking. But she'd never found herself lost in nothing but the sight of him the way she so frequently did with Noah.

Even though she hadn't actually been conscious of it, this must have been what was going on in Denver, she thought, and why she'd been susceptible enough to Noah to spend that night with him at the Expo.

But why did he have this effect on her?

Maybe it was because she'd grown up with Jack. She'd known him as a boy, as a teenager, then as a man. They'd been so familiar with each other that nothing about it had ever struck her dumb the way everything about Noah seemed to. Maybe it was just the novelty of Noah. It was the only explanation she could come up with.

"Isn't that right, Marti?"

She had absolutely no idea what Noah had said that he wanted confirmation for. None.

"Uh-huh," she muttered. Neither Noah nor Emmalina seemed to find fault with her mumbled response, but Marti knew she had to get with the program and put concerted effort into focusing her wayward attention.

"I wanted to talk to you about my grandmother," she

said as soon as there was a lull in the chitchat between Noah and Emmalina. "Noah said you remembered her?"

"Young Theresa—I remember her well. She needed someone to take her in—just a teenager with no one to look after her, her only living relative too ill to help her right away. My Charles and I talked and talked about her coming to stay with us."

"But she didn't," Marti said.

"No. Times were hard and a clergyman's pay was a pittance to feed and support our family on, so we waited, hoping someone closer to her would be able to help. Then, just when it seemed that we should offer, Hector Tyson and his wife Gloria invited her to live with them until she could go to her sick aunt."

The elderly woman frowned and shook her head. "In retrospect, Charles and I regretted that we hadn't offered her our home. In fact, it tormented Charles."

"Why?" Marti asked.

Emmalina didn't answer that and Marti could see that she was hesitant. She thought that some background on her grandmother might persuade her, so she said, "Gram mentioned that she went to see you and your first husband—the minister in Northbridge at the time. That's why I asked Noah to bring me to meet you. Whatever you and your husband said to her made a big impression."

"Oh, dear…" Emmalina muttered as if it disturbed her to discover that.

Marti went on. "Gram is scattered in her thinking—

she has emotional problems and some dementia on top of it, so it's hard to get a clear picture of what it is from her past that has her tied up in knots now. But it seems to have something to do with whatever it was she went to you and your husband to talk about. It has to do with Hector Tyson. But Gram said he told her she couldn't tell anyone and that you and your husband said the same thing, that your husband told her she had to do what was right even if it wasn't what was right for her. We want to help Gram—she keeps saying she wants us to get back what Hector took from her—but we haven't been able to figure out what that is and we wondered if you could fill us in."

Emmalina wrapped the last two tamales before she said, "I suppose I can tell you what Theresa told me." But there was obvious reluctance in her tone. "The afternoon she came to see Charles he was on an errand and while Theresa waited for him I sat with her, gave her tea and tried to just comfort her—she was so upset my heart went out to her—"

"When exactly was this?" Marti interrupted. "Was it soon after her parents died or later?"

"Later," Emmalina said, going to a cupboard for a paper sack, which she brought back to the table. As she put the tamales into the sack, she said, "This was a few months before she left town—it was in early autumn, a warm day, but Theresa was wearing a big jacket, holding it closed around her as if she was cold, and I couldn't get her to take it off."

"So she'd been with the Tysons for several months."

"Oh, yes. Since just after the holidays—she was staying with a friend's family through Christmas and Charles and I said that if she didn't have another place to go when the first of the year had come and gone, we'd try to make room for her. But that was when Hector stepped in. So yes, she'd been with the Tysons for several months."

"And she was upset the day she came to see your husband? The day you talked to her..." Marti said to remind the elderly woman what she'd been saying when Marti had interrupted her to get the timeline straight.

"Fidgety, weepy, nervous, distraught—that kind of upset, not just crying for her parents."

"What was she upset over?" Marti asked, noting that Noah was listening but letting her do the talking.

"I don't know for sure," Emmalina hedged. "She didn't tell me specifics and whatever Theresa told my husband later was between the two of them—what his flock came to him with Charles held in confidence even from me. But what Theresa *did* say to me before she spoke to Charles was that she was in love with someone she shouldn't be. That the man she was in love with was married."

"Hector Tyson?" Marti asked.

"She didn't tell me that," Emmalina hedged again, clearly not wanting to name the man when she didn't know for sure that was who Theresa had been in love with.

"But that's who you thought it was," Marti persisted.

The older woman didn't deny it, she merely continued, "Whoever it was, Theresa said that he wanted her to do something she didn't want to do, that he was telling her it was best for her to take the money he was offering her and use it to go away and start fresh. I told her that maybe that *was* best. That in my opinion she should do whatever she needed to in order *not* to break up a marriage. Then Charles came home and took her into his office and that's all I know."

Marti had the sense that there was more despite Emmalina's conclusion. So she said, "And after that?"

Emmalina shrugged and shook her head again, sadly. "Poor Theresa came running from Charles's office after about an hour, crying her little heart out. Charles found me in the kitchen and said he thought we should have Theresa move in with us right away—that day. By that point, he was as agitated as Theresa had been, so even without him giving me a reason, I agreed. I said I'd get a bed ready in Lila's room, and Charles went to get Theresa. But when he came home, he was alone. He said he couldn't convince her."

"And was that 'it?" Marti queried.

"Charles didn't give up. For more than a week he went every day to see Theresa at the Tysons. He was determined that she shouldn't go on staying with them. He even tried to get the nurse in town to have Theresa stay with her since she didn't want to stay with us. But Theresa never would go anywhere else, and finally Hector Tyson banned Charles from going to see Theresa—or even speaking to her—anymore."

"And then she left Northbridge," Marti said.

"In a few months. But without ever coming to either Charles or me again. The whole thing left my Charles tormented by guilt. He didn't say it, but I knew it was because we hadn't taken Theresa in from the start. Then, the day she left Northbridge, Charles said that he hoped the Lord didn't hold us responsible for ruining that girl's life."

Chapter Nine

Emmalina's tamales looked and smelled so good that by the time Marti and Noah left the elderly woman's house nothing sounded better for their dinner. It was Noah's suggestion that they use them as the main course for a picnic in the Town Square.

"I'm glad you like Emmalina's tamales," Noah said once they'd found a picnic table near the gazebo that was the square's centerpiece, amid the tall oak and pine trees that provided some shade.

They'd settled on opposite sides of the picnic table to eat, and Marti had tasted the tamales and decreed them spicy but delicious.

"But what did you think about what she had to say about your grandmother?" Noah asked.

That was a more complicated subject.

"I'm not sure," Marti answered honestly. "Is it better or worse that Gram might have actually loved Hector?"

Noah was unwrapping his second tamale and he raised an eyebrow in response to her question. "I'm not sure either. I guess if they loved each other, if they got carried away by their feelings but he ended up staying with his wife, it's a little more palatable than if you think he took advantage of her age and situation and seduced her without giving a damn for her otherwise."

Marti grimaced at that second scenario. "Definitely more palatable. But it's harder to believe after the things Hector said when we saw him."

Noah must have thought so, too, because he didn't respond to that. Instead, he said, "And how about that coat business?"

She knew what he was so gingerly referring to— Emmalina's comment on the oddity of Theresa insisting on keeping a big coat wrapped around her on a warm day. "It sounded like Gram was trying to hide something. Like maybe a pregnancy of her own?"

Noah's well-shaped eyebrows arched and stayed that way this time to let her know that was precisely what he'd been thinking.

"I don't know if Wyatt told you this part, but it's something my brothers and I had begun to wonder before now—if what was taken from Gram was a baby. A lot of what Emmalina said could have pointed to that."

"I thought so, too," Noah agreed without revealing

if Wyatt had let him in on their thinking. "But that just makes Hector all the bigger jerk."

Marti couldn't argue with that. She also couldn't be sure she was going to keep the tamale down suddenly.

Wrapping up what remained uneaten, she moved it out of smelling range and then drank some of her bottled water. But rather than helping, it was as if she'd poured lighter fluid on a fire and she instantly had the worst heartburn she'd ever experienced.

She tried to ignore it and said, "Did Hector and his wife have kids? I haven't heard mention of any."

"No, Hector and Gloria never had kids."

"So it wasn't as if they suddenly showed up with a baby right when Gram left Northbridge."

Noah shook his head. "Not that I ever heard."

"I don't suppose you'd know if anyone else mysteriously became parents around that time?"

"Sorry—that was twenty-six years before I was born."

When he opened his third tamale Marti's heartburn was so bad she actually recoiled slightly just at the sight.

"What?" he asked when he noticed it.

"It's nothing, just some heartburn," she downplayed. "I guess *this* baby is not a lover of spicy food."

"Uh-oh. Are we in trouble?"

Too much trouble to answer that. Marti tightly gripped the water bottle as if it anchored her and closed her eyes to keep from looking at the food he'd just unveiled. Thinking to try more water, she began to raise the bottle but Noah's hand on hers stopped it.

"Water is the last thing you want," he said.

How could she be in such misery and still be more aware of his touch than of the heartburn? She marveled as much at this reaction to him as she had earlier in Emmalina's kitchen over her inability to keep from watching him move the stove.

She opened her eyes just as he took his hand away. And somehow losing that contact with him seemed to make the heartburn even worse.

Noah looked into the grocery sack beside him on the picnic bench and produced some soda crackers. "Try these."

"I wondered why you were buying these."

"Just in case—I know how hot Emmalina makes her tamales and I thought we'd better have something to cut the heat if you couldn't take it."

Marti opened the box of crackers, took out a sleeve and began to nibble as Noah said, "Does Theresa know about our baby?"

Why did the *our* give her a tiny rush?

"No," she answered. "I haven't told her yet. I'm not sure how she'll take it, if it will upset her."

"Maybe her reaction would be a clue to her own past."

"It's impossible to say." And Marti wasn't comfortable yet with the idea of telling any of her family the truth about how her baby had come about and who its father was. Just thinking about it added stress and that made her feel even worse.

Noah must have been able to tell somehow because he made quick work of packing up their meal and stood.

"You know what? I don't think talking about your grandmother and Hector Tyson is helping anything. Come on, let's walk a little and talk about something else."

Marti was willing to try anything but she still had to smile weakly at the suggestion. "You aren't really telling me to just walk this off, are you?"

Noah laughed. "That's not what I said. Let's just see if some exercise can speed up digestion."

Marti stood, too, brushing cracker crumbs off of the brown V-neck T-shirt and tan slacks she was wearing before they went to his truck and left the grocery sack and the rest of the tamales in the back. Then they set off on the sidewalk that surrounded the Town Square.

While Marti continued to eat crackers and barely sip water when she got too dry, Noah told her about Northbridge and the old covered bridge for which it was named. The bridge had been refurbished and the area around it turned into a park to rival the Town Square. An unveiling would be held in June.

Little by little, Marti's stomach began to calm down so by the time they were back at the truck, everything was under control again, and when Noah asked if she'd like to see the bridge, she agreed—primarily so the evening wouldn't end yet.

The bridge wasn't far outside of town. Noah's description hadn't done it justice. A sharply pitched black-shingled roof topped sides that were solid on the lower half, crosshatched on the upper. It was painted a rustic red and moored by stone piers to the banks of the stream that ran below it. All around the bridge itself were freshly sodded grounds where bushes and trees had been planted.

It was beautiful and Marti told Noah so.

"If you need to walk some more we can get out and cross the bridge—it doesn't actually lead anywhere anymore but we can go back and forth," Noah offered.

"I'm okay now and I like the look of it from here, where I can get the full picture."

He'd done some of the refurbishment on the bridge and pointed out his contributions to it before he angled in his seat and started to look more at Marti than at the scenery.

And since she'd seen enough of it—and couldn't seem to get her fill of looking at him lately—she turned slightly to face Noah.

"So you're feeling better?" he asked then.

"I am."

"Better enough for some of this?" He took a large chocolate-covered mint patty from a compartment near the steering wheel and held it up for her to see.

Marti laughed. "Better enough for some of that," she confirmed.

Noah opened the foil wrapping and they each broke off a piece of the candy. Then he said, "Can I ask you something?"

"Sure."

"I'm curious. When we were first talking about your decision to have the baby you said it meant moving forward for you, that it was *life-affirming*—

that didn't seem like what most people say about a baby. But the comment that really made me wonder was when you said that there have only been two men on your dance card—me and the man you *should* be married to right now."

"Oh."

Noah picked up the sleeve of crackers she'd set on the seat, offering it to her as if what he'd said might have been enough to bring back the heartburn.

Marti laughed again. "That's okay, you haven't stressed me out that much. Yet."

He put the crackers back on the seat and they finished the mint instead. "So who's the guy you *should* be married to right now?"

Was there some jealousy echoing in that? Marti thought there might be and if the subject of Jack didn't sadden her so much she might have been flattered by the possibility that Noah was jealous of the thought of another man. As it was, sad was all she could muster.

"His name was Jack Mercer."

"And he was the *only* other guy you were ever involved with?"

"The *only* one," Marti confirmed. "We met in kindergarten, believe it or not."

"Around here that's not unheard of," he said. "Small town, remember? Any two locals who get married have known each other since they were in diapers. But sticking to that one path all the way to the altar without veering off to date someone else here and there? That's another story."

"My story," Marti said. "Jack and I were soul mates, right from the start."

"Your eyes met over the jar of paste in kindergarten class and that was it?" Noah joked.

"Kind of. It was an intense case of puppy love that became more serious over the years."

"And neither of you ever—"

"Never. Until you, Jack was the only non-relative I'd ever even kissed."

"And him?"

"Unless something happened that I don't know about—and I don't have any reason to think it did—he'd never kissed anyone but me, either."

"On purpose?" Noah asked incredulously. "I mean, I don't mean to sound so amazed, but was this some kind of blood-oath sworn to on the playground or what?"

Marti smiled. "No, Jack and I just happened. Like I said, we were soul mates."

"Joined at the hip, never hanging out with anyone else?"

"That would have been weird and it wasn't. We weren't surgically attached to each other. We had our own friends, other people we hung out with and did things with separately—I had girlfriends, Jack had guy friends, we both had brothers. But from the time Jack and I met he was who I wanted to be with—whether it was who I wanted at my birthday party or to go swimming with or who I wanted to hang out with at the mall. He was the first person I told anything to or wanted to share big news with. And I was always his choice for who to be with, who to do things with, who to talk to. It wasn't by design, it just was what it was—"

"Soul mates," Noah repeated.

Marti shrugged, wishing it didn't hurt so much to recall just how perfect she and Jack had been together, how much it had seemed as if he were her other half, as if she were only complete when she was with him. How hard it had been to find a way since his death to feel as if she were whole without him…

"It was just like this magical fluke," she went on, almost more to herself than to Noah, "that as a little kid I found the one person I was meant to be with."

"And you're sure there is *only* one person?"

Marti shrugged again. "I guess I don't know now." She hoped not, but yes, she was afraid it might be true.

"Anyway," she began again from where she'd veered from the facts. "We lived together through college, while Jack went on to get his master's degree. But we didn't want to get married until Jack was completely finished. We wanted to be less busy when it came time to plan our wedding and start our marriage. But as soon as the end was in sight, he gave me an engagement ring and we put the wheels into motion."

"And that was how long ago?"

"A year ago this last Valentine's Day. We set the wedding date for July twenty-sixth of last year."

"Which is why you *should* be married to him right now," Noah said again, making Marti wonder if that particular remark had bothered him.

She didn't ask, though, she just said, "Yes."

"Why aren't you, then?"

Even after all this time she still had to steel herself to say it.

She took a breath, pulled back her shoulders and felt something at the center of her tighten...

"Jack was killed in a car accident on his way to the church," she said, her voice very, very quiet.

Noah's eyebrows arched in shock now. And for a moment he seemed to be at a loss for words.

Then he said—also quietly but incredulously—"He was killed on the way to the *wedding?*"

Marti nodded, trying hard to tell this and not relive it, not to refeel the pain. "The minister thought I'd been left at the altar but I knew—we *all* knew—that couldn't be true. We were the perfect match, the couple everyone envied, what every friend I've ever had wanted in their own relationships. There was never anything either Jack or I wanted as much as to be together, to spend the rest of our lives together."

Noah's brows reversed directions and pulled into a frown. "What did you do? Just wait? How did you find out?"

"Of course there was a flurry of calls trying to find Jack and his older brother—who was also his best man and who was bringing Jack to the church. But we couldn't reach either of them. Then a couple of Jack's friends went looking for him and when they came back there were police with them..."

Marti's voice cracked, but she managed to keep tears

from filling her eyes by peering over her shoulder, out the windshield at the bridge again so she had something emotionless to focus on.

But from the corner of her eye she saw Noah's hands moving toward her. She knew he wanted to reach for her, maybe pull her into his arms…

Don't. If you do I'll lose it.

Maybe he heard her thoughts because he didn't reach for her. He ended up replacing his hand on the steering wheel and stretching his other arm along the top of the seat. But he did let that hand rest gently, comfortingly, around the back of her neck, and that much she could accept without losing control. In fact, it was nice…

"The police told me what had happened," Marti went on then. "Someone—probably kids—had stolen a stop sign at a bad intersection three blocks from the church. Another car hit Jack's brother's car broadside. His brother was hurt but lived. Jack was killed instantly."

The silence that followed was what usually happened so Marti knew it well. There was a moment of shock, a moment of searching for the right thing to say.

Noah whispered, "I'm so sorry, Marti."

Marti nodded, the way she'd learned to accept condolences after so much practice. "It was awful," she agreed. "I was in that same church four days later for Jack's funeral."

Noah squeezed her nape, massaging it, and she was surprised by how much it helped, how much strength his touch gave her.

Enough so that she could look at Noah again and

even force a small smile and a lighter tone to ease the tension. "How's that for satisfying your curiosity?"

Noah shook his head for a long time as if in disbelief before he said, "Nothing like what I thought."

"What did you think?"

"That you'd had a bad breakup that left you depressed or something. But this…" He shook his head again. Then he said, "So you decided to have the baby to move forward from *this?*"

"At first I thought I couldn't possibly have a baby that had come from anyone but Jack—"

Had that sounded as bad to Noah as it had to her? She didn't know. But just in case, she said, "I'm sorry, that was—"

"It's okay."

She hoped so, and took him at his word.

"But then, yes," she continued. "A baby? What could be more of an affirmation of life? And Jack was all about living life to the fullest, enjoying it, looking at it as a gift to be used well. So while this baby isn't his, I decided to think of it as a gift and an adventure and a part of life going on. Maybe even a sign that I was supposed to go on *without* Jack. On a path that truly had nothing to do with him."

Noah nodded, his eyebrows arched once more, his expression a bit forlorn—maybe at the thought that somehow he and his baby had gotten twisted up in so much that had nothing to do with him.

And Marti thought he deserved a way out of at least this dark subject.

She smiled again and said, "Okay, I've given you more than you bargained for."

The silence that fell again confirmed her impression, before Noah took the opening she'd given him to change the subject and said, "How about coming out to my place for dinner tomorrow night?"

Marti smiled. "Okay," she agreed, unreasonably glad that she hadn't scared him off by revealing her past.

Since it was late by then, they decided to call it a night, trading only small talk on the way back into town.

Then they were standing in the glow of the porch light at her grandmother's house, facing each other, and he was looking down at her very intently.

"I'm sorry if I brought up bad memories tonight," he said.

"It's okay," she assured him. And it was. Because while everyone else in her life seemed to see her as all that was left of the perfect couple, with Noah it was different. With Noah, Jack and the loss she'd suffered, her past with him, were all just one facet of her—they weren't the only things that made her up. And that was nice.

Just as it had been nice to have him help her weather the heartburn. And to have him looking at her now in that way that let her know he was seeing only her. Appreciating her. Affected in some way himself by her and being there with her…

He smiled a bad-boy smile then and said, "Great date, huh? I get you sick on tamales and then make you tell me about what had to have been the worst thing that ever happened to you."

"You do know how to show a girl a good time."

But she had had a good time with him despite everything else and suddenly all she was thinking about was the ending of the night before and that kiss they'd shared. About sharing another...

Maybe he really could read her mind, because he reached up then and brushed a strand of her hair away from her face, trailing his finger over and around her ear to end with his hand cupping her cheek. He tilted her face ever so slightly upward just as he leaned in and met her mouth with his.

His lips were parted a bit more tonight than last night, his breath was sweet from the mint they'd shared, and Marti kissed him back and tried to savor every moment.

His free arm went around her to pull her closer and rather than ending too soon, Noah deepened the kiss even more.

His lips opened wider and enticed hers, and his tongue tested the edges of her teeth, greeting hers with a seductive coyness.

Her arms went around him. His hand moved from her face to cradle the back of her head as his mouth opened even wider over hers, as his tongue plundered and claimed and made her his, kissing her until nothing existed but the two of them and that kiss that drew her in, breathing new life into her.

And even though it lasted much, much longer than any kiss that had come before it, when Noah began to put an end to it, it still wasn't enough for Marti...

But his tongue bid hers a reluctant adieu and retreated. His mouth was less forceful, his lips less parted, and then gone for a split second, back again and gone once more before they abandoned hers altogether to press against her forehead instead.

His breath in her hair was hot and just heavy enough to make it clear that he hadn't really wanted to end the kiss any more than she'd wanted him to. But now that he had, he was sticking with it.

Then she felt him take in a fortifying breath, felt his broad back and his shoulders expand, before he sighed it out as if he were giving in to something he didn't actually want to give in to.

And that was when he straightened up and away from her.

He still held her, though, as he looked down into her eyes again.

Marti watched a slow, sensual smile take that mouth she wished was lingering over hers even now.

Noah took another deep breath and kissed her again before he let her go. "I'll see you tomorrow night, then."

"Yes, you will," Marti assured him.

They exchanged good-nights and she watched him go back to his truck, drifting into the house and up to her room only after he'd driven away.

And if he'd meant to kiss her so powerfully that it would erase everything else from her mind for the first time in months, he'd accomplished it.

Because even much later, when she was lying in bed trying to sleep, it was still only Noah and his kisses she was thinking about.

Chapter Ten

Noah worked all the next day in the attic of Theresa's house, so his path crossed Marti's only once. When it did, he asked if they were still on for dinner at his place that night. Marti teased him with a "You'll have to wait and see."

So when he answered her knock on his door at seven as planned, he greeted her with a good-natured smile and said, "I'm glad you decided to come."

They were still standing at his door, though, and Marti was beginning to wonder why he hadn't asked her in. "I brought homemade chocolate chip cookies for dessert," she said, raising the plate she was carrying.

"Great. All I had planned for dessert was another stack of candy bars—I didn't know what other kinds of chocolate you like. I just figured it was a good bet you'd want chocolate for dessert."

"I eat it in any form," she told him, thinking that she might have to cut down because while she hoped it was due to the pregnancy—and even though the jeans she'd changed into tonight still fit fine—her breasts seemed to be getting bigger every day. They'd barely fit into the built-in bra of the navy blue camisole she was wearing. In fact, she was even showing a little cleavage, which had never happened when she'd worn it before.

Cleavage that Noah obviously noticed before he raised his gaze to her face again and finally let her know why he was keeping her on the porch.

"I have to warn you—I just bought this place a few months ago and I'm remodeling it. So it's kind of a mess and most of my furniture is stored in the basement. It's probably not the best time to entertain, but I hope you won't mind."

"I won't," she answered, uncommonly pleased just to be there with him.

Gone was the sweat-streaked dust and dirt, the damp hair clinging to his head from the afternoon's work. He'd showered and obviously shampooed because his rakishly untamed hair was shiny and clean, he smelled of that wonderful woodsy cologne, and how the man could look so jaw-droppingly handsome dressed in an ordinary pair of well-worn jeans and a plain black T-shirt, she would never know. But he did. Probably because the T-shirt hugged every one of those muscles she'd seen for herself that afternoon when the heat in the attic had prompted him to strip down to a tank top.

Noah ushered her in then, telling her about his newly purchased property that was almost two miles outside of Northbridge.

"I only have three acres," he was saying. "If you don't count the deck that was added a couple of years ago, the house is half a century old and needs an update, but it's still a great investment."

Marti could tell the house was in need of repair. But she could also see that the place had a lot of possibility as he led her through the living room he was obviously in the process of painting, and into a very rustic kitchen.

"Like I said, the deck is the newest thing here so I thought we could do this out back—I'm barbecuing. But let me get you something to drink before we go out there."

He poured two glasses of iced tea, which they took outside onto a huge, roofed-in redwood deck surrounded by a railing that made it an island in the sea of dirt that stretched to the old red barn.

"I'll probably plant some grass eventually and actually make some of this a real backyard," Noah explained when they stepped out onto the deck. "But as it is now it's just a barnyard and paddock for my donkey, Dilly," he said, pointing to a long-eared burro in the distance.

"You have a donkey?" Marti marveled. "For a pet? Instead of a dog or cat?"

"I don't know why not," he said, making her laugh at this other facet of him.

Marti sipped her iced tea and watched Noah raise the

lid on his barbecue so he could put two steaks on the grill, where a pan of grilled vegetables was being kept warm and what appeared to be two foil-wrapped potatoes were cooking.

When the steaks were just right Noah served them along with the grilled vegetables, the potatoes, a salad and bread.

"Contractor and master chef, too," Marti said as she cut into a succulent piece of meat.

"Hardly. If it can go on the grill and doesn't need more than salt, pepper or barbecue sauce, I'm good. Otherwise I can't cook. How about you?"

"I like to cook, actually," Marti said as they ate. "I don't do anything too gourmet, but I can use a few things other than salt, pepper and barbecue sauce."

They chatted through most of the meal about the kinds of foods they did and didn't like, but as they neared the end of dinner Marti changed the subject to venture a question that had been on her mind.

"Have you told anyone in your family about the baby yet?"

"Not yet."

"How do you think they'll react when you do tell them?"

He shrugged. "They'll be really worried for me."

Marti didn't understand that.

And it didn't sound good.

Why would his family be worried when they heard he was going to be a father? Did it mean something bad for the baby?

"Is there some sort of genetic problem? Some heredi-
tary disease that they'd be concerned about?" she asked.

"Not that I know of. Besides, I didn't say my family
will be worried about the baby. I said they'll be worried
for *me*."

"But why?" Marti persisted.

For no reason she understood, his only answer was
to raise his eyebrows at her.

Then he said, "Cookie time!"

"You can't just leave me wondering."

"How about a tour of the house?" he offered rather
than responding to that, heading for the back door with
plates in hand.

Or maybe it was just a ploy to get help cleaning up.

Because if that was what he had in mind, it worked—
Marti took the rest of the dishes with her and followed
him inside.

But she still had every intention of making him tell
her what he'd meant.

Noah continued to dodge Marti's question as he
showed her the house.

Downstairs there was the kitchen, the laundry room,
one bathroom and the living room. On the second level
there were three bedrooms and another bathroom. All
of the paint, the wallpaper, the carpeting and the light
and plumbing fixtures were dated and worn and in need
of the remodel Noah outlined for her.

Then, with Marti bringing along the plate of the
cookies she'd made, they went back out to the deck to
have dessert.

As Marti set the cookies on the table, Noah lit the candles in the center of it.

The golden glow enabled her to study him as he took a closer look at the cookies. Right there in front of her was that well-defined chest of his, those massive upper arms stretching his short sleeves taut. His chest was hidden now behind the black knit T-shirt, but something warm began to churn inside of Marti as she became completely absorbed in just looking at him…

"Chocolate chips, white chips—"

He was describing what he saw in the cookies.

Marti yanked herself out of her reverie, but it took a hefty effort.

"White chocolate, but not chips," she explained somewhat belatedly. "I like a Swiss white chocolate candy bar cut up into small pieces better than any of the chips I've found. There's also coconut and a secret ingredient I won't divulge," she said, knowing she was talking too much, overcompensating to hide her wayward thoughts.

"Not nuts," Noah said after taking a bite of one cookie. "Toffee?" he guessed.

Marti merely smiled mysteriously and tried not to think about how great-looking he was. But it was difficult because he really was great-looking and it seemed as if every time she was with him, it affected her more. *He* affected her more.

But not even that was going to keep her from pursuing the subject of how his family would react to news of the baby and she decided she'd given him enough of an opportunity to return to that subject on his own. Since he hadn't, she was going to do some probing…

"Okay, let's have it—I want to know why your family will be worried for you when you tell them about the baby."

He finished his cookie and took a second as she chose one for herself and had a bite. Neither of them were sitting at the table, though, and in what seemed like yet another delay tactic, Noah went to the deck railing instead.

He propped one hip there, raising his right foot to the rail, and leaning his back against the corner post that braced the deck roof.

Then, finally, he draped an arm over his upraised knee and said, "I have kind of bad luck when it comes to kids in my life."

"More recently than the teenage pregnancy?"

"'Fraid so."

"*How* so?" Marti asked, going to stand beside him.

"About… I guess it's been a little more than four years now, I met someone who had a son. She was divorced, she'd moved to town to start over, bought a place and hired me to do some repairs. And we hit it off. Angie Marconi. And Erik—that was her son's name. He'd just turned three when I met them and he was a little terror."

Noah smiled when he said that so Marti knew he'd enjoyed whatever terrorizing the three-year-old had done. But there was enough sadness in the smile, in his voice and in his expression to let her know this had somehow not ended much better than the teenage pregnancy.

"Erik was a character," Noah went on, reminiscing affectionately. "He had this toy tool belt and every day when I went to work he had to have it strapped on so he could follow me around and help. He'd mimic everything I did. Angie thought he might be in my way, but I was fine with it. He was so funny—it was like having entertainment while I worked."

Marti finished her cookie, hoping this story didn't end with anything bad happening to the little boy.

"Anyway," Noah went on. "Like I said, Angie and I hit it off. After Sandy in high school, I'd dated, played the field, messed around, but I hadn't gotten serious with anyone. I was kind of skittish that way. But I really liked Angie and I was crazy about Erik, and we were all a good fit. Angie wanted to take it slow—her marriage to Erik's father had ended on a sour note, she'd had a hard time of it ever since—relationships that hadn't worked out because she had a kid—and she was leery. So that's what we did—we took it slow. But still, things just got better and better and after a year, I proposed."

Marti had asked if he was married now, but for some reason it hadn't occurred to her that he might have been married before. She didn't know why it hadn't, but it hadn't.

"So you're divorced?" she asked.

Noah shook his head.

"She turned you down?"

He chuckled slightly. "No, she said yes. But she was still afraid of rushing anything so she wanted us to live together for a while."

"Did you?"

"Yeah. I moved in with her and Erik."

"And were things still okay?"

"They were great. Like I said, the three of us were a good fit. She still sort of dragged her feet about setting a wedding date but when it was getting near the two-year mark of our living together she finally decided we should plan the wedding. We also started talking about me adopting Erik."

That not only sounded somewhat ominous, but when Marti turned to lean her hip on the railing to look at Noah again she found a frown creasing his forehead and she knew this was where the bump in the road had occurred.

Then he continued. "Angie's ex had had a big-time drinking problem—that's why she'd divorced him. He hadn't paid child support or had anything to do with Erik since two months after Erik was born, so Angie didn't think there would be any problem having him relinquish his paternity rights in order for me to be Erik's legal dad. Which was how I saw myself by then—as his dad. So she tracked the ex down and went to see him to talk about it."

"But it didn't go quite as planned," Marti said in response to the deepening of Noah's voice that indicated something had gone wrong at that juncture.

"No," Noah confirmed solemnly. "When she came back she was being weird—standoffish, kind of cold, the whole first twenty-four hours that she was home she avoided my questions about her ex and the custody stuff. Then she arranged for Erik to sleep over at his friend's house the second night and said we needed to talk."

"Somehow that never seems to lead to anything good," Marti observed when he stalled.

"It didn't for me, that's for sure," Noah agreed. "She said her ex was clean and sober. That he had a job. That not only wouldn't he relinquish his parental rights, he wanted a second chance with his family."

"And she jumped at that?" Marti said in disbelief.

Noah shrugged and his expression showed some anger still, and some disbelief of his own. "She said she'd never completely gotten over her ex—which was news to me since she'd never even hinted at anything like that. But that night she said the booze had turned him into a different person during their marriage, and that now that he was sober, he was the man she'd fallen in love with again. And because Erik was his…" Noah shook his head. "She wanted them to have a second chance at being a family, too."

"And that was it for her relationship with you? For her son's relationship with you?"

Noah nodded sadly. "That was it."

"Just like that the little boy you were being a father to, who you were ready to adopt, was out the door?"

"Just like that. I tried to do something legally—to get some kind of visitation privileges or something—but essentially, I was nothing but a boyfriend, and without any biological connection, the court wouldn't grant it."

"And you really were crazy about him," Marti repeated

Noah's own words back to him, seeing what a blow it had been to him. "That must have been horrible for you."

"He *felt* like my kid," Noah admitted, staring into the night. "Erik was six by the time this happened. I'd been there pretty much from the late-baby stage. I'd taken him to his first day of kindergarten. Bought him his first big-boy bike and taught him how to ride it without training wheels."

"It was like losing your own son," Marti said for him.

"That's how it felt," he agreed in a deep, quiet voice.

"And this time it wasn't even anything you did."

"I don't know if that makes it better or worse, but no, it wasn't anything I had a part in."

Marti didn't know if that was better or worse either, and she could almost feel his frustration, his sense of helplessness...

"When did the breakup happen?" she asked quietly.

"About a year ago. So between high school, and then Erik...well, now you can understand why my family will be worried for me."

Marti nodded, knowing that if one of her brothers was in the same position, she'd be concerned, too.

"This is why you went to a lawyer the day after I told you this baby is yours, isn't it?" she guessed, recalling what he'd told her Monday night at the coffeehouse. "The teenage pregnancy and then Erik—that's why you wanted to talk about what you needed to do to protect your rights."

He turned his head to look at her, grimacing slightly

at that reminder. "Yeah. But don't forget, I didn't go through with what the lawyer suggested. It's just that like I said, I've had bad luck when it comes to kids in my life."

"You really have," Marti commiserated. "And maybe with the women in it, too."

He laughed wryly at that. "No argument there," he said. With his eyes still on her and the shadow of the past gone from them with that wry laughter, he said, "You're different from the others, though—Sandy and Angie and most of the women I've dated."

"In what way?"

"Well, for starters, you aren't sixteen. And while I'm guessing you'd like nothing better than to have a second chance for a future with Jack—that was his name, right?"

Marti nodded.

"While I'm guessing that you'd like nothing better than to have a second chance for a future with him, that isn't possible. And as for the others…" He paused with a mischievous quirk in the half smile he shot at her. "You're more the America's-Sweetheart type than beer-drinking pool shark— I dated one of those and caught her kissing another guy in a coatroom. And as far as I've seen, you aren't so obsessed with your career that you take your cell phone into the shower with you and call me by your male assistant's name at inopportune moments—"

"You dated one of those," she added for him. She could tell he was using the summary of his experiences with other women to lighten the tone and she welcomed it.

"You don't have six dogs, three cats, four birds, a

ferret and a pet iguana running around...do you?" he
went on.

"No," she laughed.

"And you had your chance to steal my wallet off the
bureau in the bedroom when I showed you around, but
you didn't."

Marti laughed again. "You *do* have bad taste in
women," she teased.

"There were some nice ones, too. Those were just the
highlights," he said with enough mischief in his smile
now to make her wonder if any of it had been true.

Then he leaned far enough over to reach her arm and
pull her to stand in front of him.

"I think my taste in women improved considerably
in Denver a couple of months ago," he said as if he were
telling her something she hadn't been involved in.
"While I was there I met this beautiful blonde with big
silver-blue eyes and skin like velvet. She had a little too
much to drink and so did I—enough to make me kind
of reckless. She let me carry her away but I knew it
wasn't something she usually did. I could tell she was
a good girl. And she was smart and sweet and indepen-
dent and a little sassy and kinda funny—"

"She sounds great," Marti joked because as nice as everything he said was, it was beginning to embarrass her.

"I think she might be," he said in a more intimate
tone as his dark brown eyes held hers. Then he pulled
her into his arms and kissed her.

In the unexpectedness of that kiss, her hands landed
on his chest and that was where they stayed—braced

by that wall of muscle she'd been admiring—as her mouth responded.

His lips parted and hers did, too—right from the start they were in sync. So much so that when his tongue came to call, hers was there ready and waiting to play.

His arms circled her, his hands clasped low on her back to pull her closer. Close enough that she was very nearly leaning against the long, massive leg that wasn't up on the railing. And while Marti fought the urge, it ran through her mind to straddle that leg. Just a little...

She didn't do it, though. She just went on kissing him back, accepting his urging to open her mouth wider, meeting his tongue and letting her own give as good as it was getting.

A soft breeze wafted around them and Marti wasn't sure if it was as cool as it felt on the bare skin of her arms and shoulders, or if she was just feeling some internal heat that made it seem that way. But what she did know was that her senses were coming alive with that kiss as she fell deeper into it.

There was an art to what he could do with that tongue, she decided as he kept at it, going from playful to teasing, from teasing to tempting, from tempting to something that was so sensual, so seductive that things were awakening inside of her that almost surprised her.

Breasts that had been sore were suddenly feeling no pain as they strained against the knit of her camisole. Her hands itched to know more than his chest, and again—the urge stronger now—she wanted to straddle that thick thigh of his...

It was only her hands she gave in to, though, letting them course outward to those remarkable biceps, riding their swells to his broad shoulders, to his strong neck and around.

One hand went to his nape while the other went to his back—every bit as solid and powerful as she'd imagined it would be.

His mouth was wide open over hers; his tongue tantalized and taunted with thrusts that made her think of things other than kissing.

He unclasped his hands and laid them flat against her back, his fingers pressed into her flesh and brought her nearer still so that her breasts met his chest. Just barely, and yet it was enough for her nipples to tighten more than she'd ever felt them tighten before. Enough to make that yearning in her body intensify beyond belief.

Her mouth opened even wider beneath his and her tongue did some thrusting of its own in a boldness that surprised her.

Maybe he'd taken that as a sign because one of his hands began to travel. From her back to her side. To the swell of her breast...

He paused there and she knew why. She knew that if she didn't want him to come the rest of the way around, he was giving her the chance to stop him.

But she didn't.

He was gentle and yet forceful. Marti felt herself expand within his grasp, flourish and strive and strain for more, hating those layers of knit that kept her from knowing the unmarred touch of his work-toughened skin.

He was kissing her with an ever-growing need and so maybe it was a craving of his own that slipped his hand up and underneath her top. But Marti wasn't the only one of them to breathe a hot gust of excited breath when skin finally met skin.

If the feel of that kneading, caressing hand on her breast had been wonderful before, it was nothing compared to this! She'd never felt anything as good and the quiet moan that escaped her throat, the arch of her back, the diamond-hard cresting of her nipple into his palm must have let him know because he was plundering her mouth with his tongue and his arm around her pulled her up against him so tight that she had no choice but to do that one thing she'd been trying not to give in to—his leg came between hers.

And when it did he bent his knee. Only enough to bring his thick thigh up against her and teach her that it wasn't only her breasts that pregnancy had made more keenly sensitive…

He hadn't been lying when he'd said there wasn't much furniture in his house. But there was a bed in his bedroom—she'd seen it. And suddenly that was all she could think about—having him take her there, tearing off his clothes, letting him tear off hers, making love that wouldn't only be a vague, hazy memory that didn't seem like it had really happened.

Should she or shouldn't she?

Should she or shouldn't she…

Oh, how she wanted to!

She pressed a little more on his leg.

He raised that thigh a little more to meet her.

They'd already spent one night together—even if she couldn't really remember it, it *had* happened. They were having a baby to prove it. Why couldn't she have another night with him…

But it was the thought of that baby that put a damper on things for her.

That baby was their only real tie, she thought suddenly. Their only real connection.

If not for that baby, they wouldn't be here at all, let alone like this. And maybe that wasn't enough to let this happen again.

This time when her hands moved on their own it was to his chest to push herself away from that kiss, from him.

He got the message, too, and his hands dropped to her hips. "If you're not comfortable, there *are* a few alternatives to being out on the deck," he said with a nod toward the house.

Marti sighed. "That's what I'm afraid of."

"You're *afraid* of me?" he asked, his voice deep and ragged. "Because you know there's nothing to be afraid of here."

She did know that. "Maybe I'm afraid of myself," she confessed quietly.

Noah's dark eyes searched hers for a long while and she thought he knew that it wouldn't take much persuasion for her to change her mind.

But in the end he respected her wishes and just nodded.

He also used his hands at her hips to move her farther away from him before he dropped his foot to the floor and took a very deep breath.

"So…" he said on the exhale. "Chess? Checkers? Scrabble? A movie? What can I interest you in if not me?"

Marti smiled. "It's getting late, I think I should head for home." Especially since she was sure that if she stayed for any reason she wasn't going to be able to resist him.

He nodded again and merely followed her as she took the lead to leave.

He walked her to her car but Marti made certain not to take long getting in because she knew if she let him kiss her again she'd be lost.

He closed the door after she'd gotten behind the wheel and with both hands hooked over the open window, he peered in at her.

"I'll see you tomorrow," he said.

"You're working on a Saturday?" she asked, relieved to hear it because it had just occurred to her that she didn't know when she was going to see him again.

"My boss is tough," he joked.

"I've heard that," she said facetiously, hoping he might kiss her again in spite of the fact that she'd given him every indication that he wasn't supposed to.

But then he shoved off the SUV and hit the roof.

"Tomorrow," he said.

Marti took a turn at nodding. "Tomorrow," she countered, starting the engine and putting it into gear even as she was willing him to lunge through that window, to kiss her just once more…

She even tipped her chin to look at him, to give him the opportunity, to let him know she was having second thoughts about leaving.

But rather than stepping forward, Noah stepped back, getting out of the way.

Marti merely smiled a smile she hoped didn't show her second thoughts or her regrets, and let the SUV roll slowly in reverse.

And even though he waved goodbye to her, she had the feeling that he was working out some frustration.

Or maybe it was her own frustration that made it seem like that.

Because what she really wanted to do was forget everything else and let him take her to bed again after all.

Chapter Eleven

"Oh! Noah! Come quick!"

"It's all right, Gram. It's nothing…" Marti tried to assure her grandmother Saturday night when a bad dizzy spell turned the room upside down and caused Marti's knees to buckle. She'd stumbled against the coffee table, reeled around and ended up sitting on it, in the middle of the game they'd been playing.

But despite Marti's attempts to keep her grandmother from being frightened, Theresa went on shouting frantically for Noah who came running from the kitchen.

"What's the matter?"

"Nothing," Marti said unconvincingly as she suffered through the awful light-headedness and nausea and inability to see straight.

"*Something* is wrong!" Theresa insisted. "Look at her! She dropped the dice and got up to get them and all of a sudden her face went pale and she sat right on the Monopoly board! She's sick!"

"I'm not sick…"

Noah dropped down onto his haunches in front of her and took her hands in his. She could focus just enough to see that he was concerned but calm and in control, ready to do whatever needed to be done.

"Dizzy," Marti confided in him to let him know there was nothing that *needed* to be done. "Scared Gram. But really…nothing…"

"What can I do for you? How about a glass of water? Do you want to lie down?" he asked as Theresa began to rock back and forth in a frenzy.

"It'll pass. Take care of Gram," Marti said even though she liked having Noah there for her. But Theresa had had a particularly bad day. She'd been disoriented and depressed, she'd refused to eat, she'd sobbed through most of the afternoon. It was why Marti had had to turn down Noah's invitation to the Spring Fling dance in town tonight. Why—together with Mary Pat—they'd all been trying to keep Theresa occupied. It was even why Mary Pat had gone to get ice cream when Theresa had asked if they had any in the house—every effort was being made to pull Theresa out of a worse-than-usual funk and Marti knew alarming her easily excitable, fearful grandmother was not going to aid that cause.

"Really, I'm okay," she told Noah when he stayed with her.

He hesitated a moment more but then took Marti at her word, squeezed her hand and stood to deal with her grandmother.

"It's okay, Theresa. Marti just got a little dizzy. She must have stood up too fast—you've done that before, haven't you?" he said in a voice that made light of the situation.

But apparently Theresa wasn't convinced. "I think she's sick," the older woman insisted, her agitation clearly growing. "Should we call a doctor? Should you take her to the hospital? Mary Pat is a nurse. She would know!"

"Mary Pat just went for ice cream, remember? She felt like getting a little air while we finished our game," Noah reminded her. "She'll be back any time and until then, I don't think we need a doctor or—"

"Gram, it's all right," Marti managed when Theresa was not reassured. "I'm pregnant," she added, hoping that rather than upsetting her grandmother more, the news might alleviate some of the fretfulness and worry for Marti's health. "The baby just makes me dizzy sometimes. It'll pass. It always does."

There was silence in the room for a moment and although Marti was still having some difficulty seeing, she knew she'd stunned her grandmother.

Then, just as the vertigo began to pass, Marti heard Theresa say, "You're going to have a baby? But you aren't married, are you?"

Marti swallowed hard. "No, you're right, I'm not married," she confirmed because she could hear that Theresa was becoming muddled.

"It's Hector again, isn't it?" Theresa said in even more panic and confusion. "Don't let him take your baby, Marti! Don't listen to him! He says he loves you but he won't leave his wife. He says take the money and go somewhere where no one will ever know but if you let him take the baby you'll be sorry! You'll never even know if it's a boy or a girl or where it is or what happened to it! You'll be so sorry! So sorry, Marti…"

It was Marti's turn to be stunned. And maybe that was what made the dizziness hit her again. Or maybe it was the regret for having set Theresa off even if it had finally revealed some of what Theresa had been refusing to tell anyone until now.

All Marti could get out in response was another "Gram…" before she had to stop because a wave of nausea threatened and her head was so light she started to worry that she was going to faint.

Noah must have realized she'd relapsed because he put a steadying hand on her shoulder and said, "Take a deep breath. Can you put your head between your knees?"

She recoiled at the suggestion because she knew if she tried to put her head between her knees she really would lose her dinner. "I'm fine," she barely whispered. "Just take care of Gram. Get her out of here, maybe…"

"You're sure?" he asked dubiously.

Marti nodded. "Go."

Noah squeezed her shoulder this time and she heard him say, "You know what, Theresa? I hung your porch swing and you still haven't been out to see it. It's late and there's no one around and it's nice outside—why don't you and I go take a look at it now and just let Marti relax a little?"

"But the baby! Hector—"

"I'm gonna tell you a secret."

Through her skewed vision, Marti saw him take her grandmother's hand and place it in the crook of his elbow where he kept his own hand over it. He leaned close to Theresa's ear.

"Marti's baby is mine," he confided. "Hector doesn't have anything to do with it and I won't let him anywhere near it."

His voice was soothing and it wasn't only Theresa it was helping. Marti's dizziness began to let up, too.

"But what about *my* baby, Noah?" Theresa asked pitifully. "Can you make Hector tell you what he did with it? I want it back. That's why I came home here— to get back my baby that Hector took."

"You know, Theresa, I understand how horrible that was for you. How you feel—"

"You do?"

"I honestly do. And I promise you that I'll help Marti and Ry and Wyatt do whatever it takes to make it right for you. But we can't do anything tonight. So let's just go out on the porch and see your swing, and give Marti a minute to take some deep breaths and settle down a little. Then I'll bet she'll come out and sit with us. What do you say?"

Theresa rarely went out of the house and there was hesitation now.

But just as Marti was sure a refusal was coming, her

grandmother seemed to gain some semblance of peace and said, "I did always love having a porch swing."

"I know. You told me last week—remember? That's why I put it up. I'd have my feelings hurt if you didn't go out and at least take a look at it."

And to Marti's amazement, her grandmother went outside with Noah.

An hour after Marti's dizzy spell on Saturday night—and her impromptu announcement to her grandmother that she was pregnant—her symptoms were gone. She felt fine.

She'd dished out ice cream when Mary Pat brought it home, then helped her grandmother's nurse get Theresa settled in for bed, and said good-night to Mary Pat, who had gone to bed, too.

So as Marti returned to the porch, all was calm and quiet.

And Noah was waiting patiently for her.

"Are you mad at me?" he asked as soon as she went out the front door.

He was sitting crossways on the wooden swing that he'd used to lure her grandmother from the house. One long, jean-clad leg ran the length of the seat while his other foot was flat on the porch floor. His arms were stretched along the top of the seat back and side so that the white shirt he was wearing, with the sleeves rolled to his elbows, was smooth across his perfect torso.

"Mad at you? Are you kidding?" she asked as she went to the swing where she swept into a mock curtsy.

"I bow to your greatness—how you actually had my grandmother laughing by the time I got out here earlier is a mystery. What would I be mad at you for after that?"

Noah reached for her hand and—much as he'd done the night before on his deck—pulled her toward him. Only tonight he didn't stop at merely bringing her near; she ended up on the swing between his legs with her back to his chest.

He wrapped one arm around her and with his other hand, he held her head to his shoulder. And while she wasn't sure if it was the smartest thing she'd ever done, she brought her own denim-encased legs up onto the seat and hooked her hands around his forearm, resting there as comfortably as if it was something she'd done hundreds of times, feeling surprisingly natural there, like that, with him…

"I thought you might not be too happy that I told your grandmother the baby is mine," he said then.

"Oh, that… No, I'm not mad. How could I be when I'd just blurted out that I'm pregnant and upset her more than she'd been in the first place?"

"So much for waiting for the right moment, huh?"

"It just seemed like it might help if she knew nothing serious was happening. But clearly *that* was not the wisest choice. And since telling her the baby is yours helped mellow her out, it's probably good that you did it."

"But you aren't thrilled."

"It's okay. I would have rather told my brothers first. But you never know with Gram, she might not even remember it tomorrow. Look what happened when I told her I was pregnant—she confused the past with the present, herself and me, and she threw Hector into the mix on top of it."

Noah paused a beat before he said, "Yeah, what do you think about all that?"

Marti shrugged and it felt so good to rub against him that, even through the scoopneck taupe T-shirt she was wearing, it turned her on.

Not that she wanted to be turned on.

We're talking about Gram, forget everything else, she commanded herself.

"I know the things she said *could* be delusional—all or just part of it," Marti answered his question. "There's always that possibility. Sometimes she watches a movie or a television show and the next day she thinks it happened to her. But this... I don't know, it seemed real."

"Especially when you consider what Emmalina told us," Noah pointed out.

"I know. Then it really does seem as if Gram just confirmed what we've suspected—that she *did* have an affair with Hector Tyson, that she got pregnant, that she had the baby and that Hector took it from her after it was born and made her leave town."

"Right," Noah agreed, dropping his chin to the top of her head.

"There are still so many questions, though," Marti said, trying not to snuggle into him. And failing a little. "Did the affair go on right under Hector's wife's nose? I think Gram had feelings for Hector—whether they were real or it was just a crush—but what about Hector? *Did* he love her? Or is he so much of a jerk that he just pretended he did to seduce her and get his hands on her land? And what about the baby?"

"I wonder if we could find out and maybe get Theresa together with her long-lost kid."

Marti glanced up at Noah, at his chiseled features gilded by the porch light. "You meant that promise to her?"

"Did you think I was lying?"

"I guess at that point I thought you might say anything to get things under control."

"I don't make any promises I don't intend to keep. Although I'll leave it to you and your brothers to tell me what I *can* do to help."

"I want to talk to Hector again, that's for sure," Marti decreed.

"And I don't want you anywhere near him alone, so I'll definitely be going with you."

Marti smiled and let herself bask for a moment in that bit of protectiveness, appreciating it. But then, there had been a lot of things she'd appreciated about him tonight.

"You really have redeemed yourself and become a good guy, haven't you?" she said.

He dipped his chin to gaze down at her. "I'm doing my damnedest," he said with just enough mischief in his tone to wash away any notion that he was *too* good.

"What about you?" he asked then, as if he didn't want to dwell too long on himself. "How do you feel?"

"I *am* okay. The dizziness comes and goes, and when it goes, it's gone—it's back to business as usual."

But despite that reassurance, Noah said in a deep, solemn voice, "I don't like to see you sick."

Marti smiled. "It could be worse—I had a friend who threw up day and night for the whole nine months. *That* was sick."

"I still don't like it."

"Then tell your kid to cut it out," she suggested with a laugh.

He took his hand from caressing her head to lay his palm on her stomach, surprising her.

"Cut it out, kid," he said as the warmth of that big hand infused her.

She'd managed to keep her arousal at bay until that. But the weight of his hand set it off with a vengeance.

It didn't seem to be only her, though. There was suddenly something passing between them, something that didn't have anything to do with what they'd been talking about. With her grandmother, or even with the baby. Something that was only about the two of them.

Marti turned slightly in his arms and tipped her head farther back to get a better look at him.

He peered down at her, his dark eyes reflecting the same pure, raw desire that was running through her body, that had been awakened in her the night before.

"Are you gonna kiss me or what?" Marti whispered when he just went on searching her face and it seemed as if he might not.

Noah smiled and dropped his head to capture her

mouth with a kiss that was smooth and sexy right from the start.

Marti pressed a hand to the solid wall of his chest but that wasn't the only thing she felt as that kiss deepened and their mouths opened wider. Near her hip there was another hardness that told her for sure that she wasn't the only one who'd been left on simmer since last night…

But Noah pulled away. "I better get out of here. I want you so damn bad, Marti, that if I don't go right now…"

He didn't finish that. And he didn't move.

And neither did she.

Because she wanted him so damn bad, too…

She sat up and kissed him again, knowing she shouldn't, that she was only making matters worse for them both. But she just couldn't help herself.

And that was when the wheels of her mind began to spin. When she realized that what had stopped her the previous evening had been the thought that nothing connected them except the baby.

But maybe this was more a need for connecting than connection. For satisfying an intense and abiding desire to be with this man as closely and as intimately as she possibly could be. And maybe that purely elemental drive was all she had to consider right now.

Certainly that was all that seemed to matter to her.

So why couldn't she give in to it?

She couldn't think of a reason why she couldn't. Not when she wanted to. When she wanted to so much…

It was Marti who ended that second kiss. "I don't want you to go at all tonight."

Noah's eyebrows arched toward his hairline. "No?"

"No," she confirmed.

"Oka-ay... But shouldn't we go back to my place or something?"

She shook her head. She couldn't wait that long. And she knew that he was fully aware that she'd turned the downstairs den into her room because he'd moved her double bed there first thing that morning.

"No one upstairs can hear anything. That's why I moved into the den—so I wouldn't disturb Gram or Mary Pat when I'm up late."

"And tonight you're not afraid of doing this?" he asked, echoing what she'd said when she'd stopped this same thing on his deck the night before.

She really wasn't, though. She'd spent last night frustrated and unconvinced that she'd done something that had to be done by not making love with him. She'd spent hours thinking, *What real harm would there have been...*

And she hadn't come up with an answer then, any more than she had just now. Tonight she just wanted *him* and nothing about that seemed wrong.

"The only thing I'm afraid of is not getting behind closed doors," she joked.

He grinned. "Then by all means..."

He swung them off the seat, taking her hand to lead her into the house as if it were his.

Since he was remodeling the place, he knew it as well as Marti did. He locked the front door behind them and took her to the den, where he closed that door behind them, too. He didn't turn the light on, though—

only moonglow lit the way as he crossed to her bed and stopped at the foot of it to pull her into his arms again and kiss her.

Not that Marti had any complaints. She was as eager, as demanding, as hungry for him as he was for her.

Hungrier, maybe, because her hands went instantly to the buttons of his shirt, unfastening them so she could pull the tails of it from his jeans and get it off of him.

Marti told herself not to rush, just to enjoy. Slowing herself down, she pressed her hands to his now-naked chest, reveling in the feel of sleek flesh over toned muscle, pleased by the response of his nipples to her teasing fingers.

His tongue staked a claim and left no doubt who was boss while Marti went on trailing her fingers over his broad shoulders, biceps and that Herculean back.

His hands dropped away from her then—away from her face, away from her breasts—and came together at the waistband of her jeans. But still he didn't undo the button. Instead he just held on—the backs of his fingers dipping inside her pants and panties only slightly— while he kicked off his shoes.

Marti was only wearing sandals and she'd already stepped out of them, but she liked the idea of her hands in his jeans, too, so she slipped them to the small of his back, hooked her thumbs in his waistband and came around.

He didn't have quite so much leeway at the front of his, though, since he was nearly burgeoning out of them.

Delighted by that proof, she undid his button and the

zipper opened with very little help. That was when she dished out a little torturous restraint of her own and let her hands drift back up his washboard abs to his pecs again.

Nothing was lost on Noah, who chuckled in the midst of kissing her. But things sped up from there.

His mouth abandoned hers just as he unhooked her bra from outside of her T-shirt so he could pull shirt and bra up and off together and fling them aside. Down went her jeans and panties in unison, too, leaving Marti suddenly naked before him.

Then he turned her to face the bed, dropping his mouth to the slope of her neck and onto her shoulder to kiss and nibble and flick the tip of his tongue there while he divested himself of the rest of his clothes. When he had, his arms came around her to lay both of his palms on her belly, bringing every nerve ending to the surface of her skin, shivering, leaving her wilted against him, the evidence of how much he wanted her standing long and hard between them.

Up went both his hands to her breasts then, cupping them, caressing them, molding them gently in a firm grip that made Marti breathe in a whole new way, that made her head fall back against him, her eyes close, her mouth go slack...

But just when she was lost to that tender exploration, Noah was gone, then back again to lift her as if she weighed nothing and set her on the bed. He joined her so that the front of his body ran the length of her side.

His mouth reclaimed hers as his hand reached her

bare, engorged breasts once more, satisfying her renewed craving for his touch.

Stroking, kneading, massaging—he was a maestro, orchestrating a symphony of pleasures with his fingertips. His lightest touch sent her into a near frenzy.

But as spectacular and arousing as it was, when his mouth again left hers and replaced his hand, spectacular didn't describe it. Her spine arched off the quilt that covered her bed and a tiny involuntary groan escaped her throat as his magic fingers slid down her stomach and between her legs.

Marti nearly came completely off the bed as Noah found every sweet spot there was to be found and awakened them all at once.

She turned to her side, letting her leg go over his hip and finding that steely staff with her own hand to encourage him into the same kind of frantic need he was building in her.

Urgency mounted. Noah drew his fingers out of her with exquisite slowness and then coursed around to her rear, pulling her into the perfect position for him to ease into her.

How she could ever have lost any portion of any memory of how fantastic that felt, Marti didn't know. But Denver was nothing—tonight was fresh and new and more exciting than she could ever have imagined. In that instant she was lost to the act, to the man, to each divine movement he initiated and guided all the while his hands explored every inch of her flesh so erotically he nearly drove her out of her mind.

Slowly at first, he rocked them together, into her and out, rhythmically, skillfully increasing the speed, the intensity, being cautious until caution wasn't possible. Until passion and need took control.

Faster then, harder, deeper. Marti clung to him, moved with him, held him to her, clutching him, her fingers digging into his broad, powerful back.

And when she reached the pinnacle of it all it was an explosion of ecstasy that suspended her in the circle of his arms, against the magnificence of his body, merging more than physically with him as he also found his peak and pushed so deeply within her they seemed to fuse together.

They were both breathing hard. Marti's heart was beating fast and she could feel that Noah's was, too. And for a moment there was only the two of them winding down from what had been nothing less than profound.

They held each other as closely as possible, and that was how they stayed even as Noah rolled to his back and took her with him to lie on top of him as if she were hugging a big body pillow, her head resting on his chest, him still inside of her.

"Are you okay?" he asked then, his voice passion-ragged but sounding a little alarmed. "I meant to be more careful but—"

"I'm fine," Marti assured him. "Not even dizzy."

He laughed, a low rumble beneath her. "Then maybe I didn't do my job."

"This was work?"

"Ooh, only the best kind..." he moaned, making her laugh as well.

Then he said, "You really are all right? I didn't hurt anything?"

"I really am all right."

He sighed, relieved. "Good."

Sooo good...

"Do you want me out of here?" he asked.

It took her a moment to realize he was talking about the house, not her.

"No. Do you want out of here?" she countered.

"Never," he said, pulsing inside of her as if he might have meant her after all. "But what about your roommates?"

"They'll be asleep for hours and hours and hours," Marti said wearily as an overwhelming fatigue suddenly washed through her.

"Then can I stay until just before we might get caught?"

"I think you're going to have to... I don't think I can move..." she said softly, her words slow, her voice heavy.

She felt Noah crane forward a little for a look at her before he settled back again and said, "Hey, it's supposed to be the guy who can't stay awake at this point."

But his comment was only a joke because he laughed again, rubbing her back and only making it more difficult for her not to drift off.

"Mmm," was all Marti could manage in answer and in response to that backrub.

Noah reached to the side, grabbed what he could of the quilt and brought it over her.

"Sleep, then," he said. "I'm sorry I wore you out."

Marti wanted to welcome him to wear her out again in a little while.

But she was just too comfortable and too, too tired to do anything but give in to the pull of slumber in his arms.

Chapter Twelve

Sunday's sun was just rising over the horizon after the third time Noah made love to Marti. She had again fallen asleep almost immediately and even though Noah was in the same exhausted state by then, he knew he couldn't give in to it. He had to leave before Theresa or Mary Pat woke up.

So he forced himself to ease his arms from around the snoozing Marti and got up.

He dressed in no time and then went to sit on the edge of the bed beside her.

"I'm gonna go," he said in a quiet voice.

"Mmm… Wish you didn't have to," Marti responded thickly without opening her eyes.

"I'll come back later, okay?"

"Good."

And she was gone again.

Noah stayed where he was, though, watching her sleep, stroking the side of her face with the backs of his fingertips.

God, she was beautiful.

Her honey-and-cream-colored hair fanned out against the pillow. Her red lips were slightly parted, as if she were about to blow a kiss. Her long, thick lashes rested against pale, flawless skin, and it was all he could do not to lie down beside her again, take her back into his arms and never leave.

He sighed heavily as that thought went through his mind, as that potent feeling took hold of him.

He didn't *ever* want to leave Marti. Or their baby.

Something else flashed through his mind just that quick—an image of himself and Marti genuinely together, as a couple, as a family with their baby, and in one moment of absolute clarity he knew without a doubt that that was what he wanted.

What he didn't know was if Marti would want the same thing.

He knew she wanted the baby. And through the night she'd wanted him, too. But what about from here on?

She wasn't completely unplugged from her past, from her first love, and Noah knew it. And it was a formidable past for him to be up against.

But just how much *was* he up against? Did she still love the other guy so much there wasn't room for anyone else? Would she *ever* be completely over the other guy? *Could* she be? Or would he always be runner-up even if she did let him into her life the way he wanted to be?

And if there were always three of them in the relationship—Marti, her late fiancé and him—what would that be like? Could he handle it?

But when Noah thought about it like that, he knew that when he and Marti were together he didn't have the feeling that there was a ghost lurking between them. Sure, when Marti talked about Jack, Noah knew he was in her head, in her heart. But when she wasn't talking about him, it felt like her focus was solely on whatever *they* were talking about or doing. On him.

And in bed?

Noah had had some experience with a woman distracted by things other than him and that was definitely not Marti. It hadn't been true in Denver six weeks ago and it sure as hell hadn't been true last night.

Marti might not see him as her soul mate—the way she'd seen Jack—but there was something strong enough between them to make Noah believe that he had a place in her life, too.

And, hopefully, in her heart.

As he sat there watching her sleep, knowing he should leave, he hoped it was more than possible. That he might even have already begun to take the lead over the other guy.

Because the more he thought about it, the more he wanted her, the more he wanted them to have this baby together, raise it together. The more he wanted them to have a life—a whole, full life—to have other kids and a house and a dog and holidays and birthdays and vacations together. To reach milestones, to weather storms, to ride out every high and low, to be together for the rest of their lives no matter what those lives brought.

But what if…

What if he told Marti what he wanted and she balked?

She was still rough around the edges, he knew that. And that made her more unpredictable. And that unpredictability increased the risk if he pushed. Especially since this had all happened so fast—one night in Denver, only a week in Northbridge.

He didn't think she would change her mind about having the baby, but if trying for so much more now turned her off, she could make it tougher for him to have a part in the baby's life. He could be left in the court battle he'd been trying to avoid just to be granted any rights at all. Or he could lose the court battle, lose both Marti and the baby and end up with nothing.

Just the way he'd lost out twice before.

And as bad as that had been both of the other times, the thought of it happening now, with Marti, with this baby, was even worse.

So maybe he should just keep his mouth shut, he told himself. Maybe he should let things stay the way they were and hope for the best.

But what was the best he could hope for if he didn't push for more?

That he'd see Marti when she came into town periodically? That he'd see her now and then if he could swing the time for a few days in Missoula? That he'd only see his son or daughter then and that way, too?

And what if Marti met someone else along the way—because there was that possibility, too. It wasn't as if he'd be occupying her every minute and what if some other guy she met in Missoula caught her interest? Someone who would have more chance than he did to be with her. Someone who would have more chance than he did to be with his kid.

I'd be so far in the outfield I wouldn't even be in the game...

He couldn't stand that thought.

Dealing with the ghost of Marti's late soul mate was one thing—it might not be easy, but it was a hell of a lot easier than trying to scrape together a few crumbs with her and with his son or daughter if they ended up becoming a family with someone else.

He just couldn't let that happen. He couldn't.

But he *could* wait a little, he told himself. He could wait and hope that whatever it was that had been between them in Denver and then reignited here in Northbridge would flourish, would lead them where he wanted them to end up.

He could have patience, he told himself. And practicing patience was probably a wiser idea.

But it didn't make a damn bit of difference.

Because as he sat there, staring down at Marti, wanting her so much it made him ache, he knew patience was beyond his grasp. Especially now that the image of someone else ending up with her was in his head.

Noah was already waiting for her when Marti pulled up in front of Hector Tyson's house Sunday afternoon. He'd called around noon to tell her he wanted to see her today and she'd suggested they waste no time confronting Tyson about Theresa's accusations.

Noah had said he would rather talk to her first but still he'd conceded to arrange the meeting.

"And maybe afterward we can talk," he'd said.

He stood watching Marti as she brought her brother's SUV to a stop right behind him. His long legs were stretched out in front of him as if he'd been there for a while, his hands were in his jean pockets. He was wearing a plain beige sport shirt with the sleeves rolled to mid-forearm. His hair glistened with a freshly washed sheen in the May sunshine and his angular face was clean-shaven. And when Marti turned off her engine and got out to walk over to him, she had to fight the urge to fling herself into his arms and pick up where they'd left off the night before.

But she managed to contain herself, merely smiled and said a simple, "Hi."

He smiled back as if he were glad to see her, but there was something else around the edges of his smile that she couldn't figure out. Something that looked as if he were holding back, too, but maybe not in the same way or for the same reason she was.

"Have you been waiting long?" Marti asked him after he returned her greeting.

"Nah, only a few minutes. Hector isn't home yet, though. We're catching him after his Sunday brunch and he'll keep us waiting—he was none too happy to see you again but I told him he didn't have a choice."

"Are you sure he'll show at all?"

"He has to come home sometime," Noah reasoned.

Marti had joined him at his truck, wishing mightily that he would take his hands out of his pockets and reach for her, pull her to him and kiss her—even if they were out in the open.

But he didn't and instead she was left merely standing in the vicinity of his knees, drinking in the sight of him and remembering vividly every minute of their night together.

"I'm sorry you had to slink out so early this morning," she said then, wondering if she'd been able to sleep in his arms the way she'd wanted to, to wake up in them, to linger in bed with him this morning, if it would have helped the cravings she was feeling now.

"It's okay. I would have rather stayed, but… Well, it opened my eyes to something."

For some reason Marti couldn't pinpoint, that didn't sound altogether good.

"Did it even open your eyes to how much nicer it is to have your own place and not have to worry that someone's grandmother is going to catch you?" she joked.

He chuckled. "That, too," he agreed, but even though he'd accepted her bit of levity he still went on looking at her with a penetrating, searching gaze. "Can I ask you something while we wait here?"

"Sure."

"Why me?"

"Why you what?" she asked in return, confused.

"You said that until me you'd never even kissed anyone besides Jack. So why me? And why not only kissing but everything else we did that night in Denver?"

"This is about Denver?" Marti said.

Noah shrugged. "I'm just wondering."

"I was comfortable with you," she said, trying to sort through it. "You were easy to talk to and funny." And hard to take her eyes off of, but she didn't say that.

What she did say was, "I liked you and being with you was… I don't know— I'd gone to the Expo because my whole world had become about losing Jack, about grief, and I needed to break out of that. And there you were. You didn't know any of it and you didn't treat me with kid gloves and that was nice. *You* were nice and being with you…" Marti shrugged. "Being with you made me feel better than I had in a long time. It made me feel alive again, I guess. And normal. And as if there was more to me than just Jack and what we'd had together and what we never would have together now, and that was kind of freeing. Is that bad?"

Noah shook his head. "I think that's all good. Doesn't it seem good to you—that being with me can bring you out of a tough time? That it can make you feel better and have fun again and go on with your own life and be normal?"

"Yes?" she agreed tentatively because she had the feeling she was being set up.

"So even though we don't have a history the way you did with Jack, wouldn't you say that there's something here? Between us?"

"Something," she allowed, again not committing to too much because she didn't know where this was going.

"Something besides the baby, *more* than the baby?"

She wasn't sure of that but when she hesitated to answer, Noah added, "Something we could build on?"

"Is this what you wanted to talk about?" she asked rather than answer him.

"Yeah."

"Just because you had to leave this morning?"

"I didn't want to go. But not just this morning. I didn't want to have to go at all. Ever."

That was heartening to hear, but it also made her uneasy because she thought she was beginning to see where he was headed with this.

Marti didn't say anything to that and Noah went on anyway. "You know, sometimes people who are going to have a baby get married."

"Sometimes," she allowed, but that was what she'd been afraid this could be leading to. That everything he'd just said had only been laying the groundwork. That this—the baby—was really what he was thinking about.

"When I was a teenager in this position," he went on, "I thought that that's what should be done—that Sandy and I should get married."

"I know, you told me. But you were a *teenager* who didn't recognize the reality of marriage."

"Now I'm older and I'm wondering if it would be such a bad idea for you and me."

He was tiptoeing around this and Marti didn't know if it was because marriage was something he thought he should offer even though he wasn't sold on it himself, or because he was worried about her reaction.

"I think marriage should never be a have-to," she said.

"I'm not saying have-to."

"Getting married because there's a baby on the way is a have-to," she persisted.

"What about getting married because we're good together *and* there's a baby on the way?" he said.

Then, before Marti could respond, he said, "I know there's no competing with a childhood sweetheart who was also a soul mate, somebody who was the *only* person you ever pictured yourself with. But there *is* a baby and I just got to thinking that maybe because there is, you could…readjust your vision of things."

He said that conversationally, as if he was just throwing a hypothetical idea out onto the table for her to consider. And Marti wasn't sure if there was more to it than that or not.

"Readjust my vision of things to include us getting married?" she reiterated.

"Sure. Why not? No, I'm not Jack, but I think we have something, Marti. Something out of the ordinary already." He splayed his fingers to his chest for emphasis. "I feel it. Don't you? Didn't you last night?"

"I felt a lot of things last night, but—"

"But what?" he said, seizing that word as if she'd cracked a door open and he was pushing through it. "We're good together—in bed and out of it—that's more than a lot of people can say. I'm who you picked—the one person—to help put a stop to your grieving, to get back into life with. To be *able* to get back into life with. I'm who you picked to move on with, so let's keep it moving. You're having *my* baby. I want us to raise it together and I think we should get married to do it."

By the end of that Noah was too impassioned for Marti to think he was merely suggesting marriage as a fleeting thought or even because he felt obligated to.

But it also left her seeing what she thought was the real reason behind his less-than-traditional proposal— he was afraid of losing this baby the way he'd lost the other children he'd wanted so badly.

And while she saw his point of view, all she could do was shake her head in denial.

"It's okay," she assured him. "We don't have to be married for you to have as big a part as you want in the baby's life. You won't lose this one—"

"That's not true," he said, the emotion still in his voice. "You'll be in Missoula, so that's where he or she will be while I'm here—I won't have any part as long as we're on separate sides of the state. And if you hook up with somebody else on top of it—"

"So this is a *preventative* proposal?"

"No," he said. He shook his head and stared down at

the ground as if he were regrouping. "Maybe I'm not handling this well," he added more to himself than to her.

Then he looked at her again, his dark eyes penetrating and troubled, and when he spoke once more the emotions were better under control. "Yes, I'm afraid of losing the baby. But I'm just as afraid of losing you. It's you I'm proposing to, not the baby, not even the mother of my child. Just you."

"But if there wasn't a baby we wouldn't be here," she felt compelled to remind him, to refute that.

"I think we might be. We still would have had the night in Denver—that's where this started, don't forget. You still would have come to Northbridge for your grandmother. We still would have met up again. And believe me, I still hadn't stopped thinking about you even though Denver was weeks behind me, so the minute I set eyes on you when you showed up here, I would have been doing my damnedest to spend time with you, to get to know you. We could easily have still ended up—"

"I don't believe that."

"Why? Why couldn't that have been our story? Just because we didn't grow up together, just because I didn't give you your first kiss and you didn't give me mine?"

"Just because it isn't likely," she said.

"It happens all the time—people know instantly that they're right for each other," he said, his tone intense again.

"You're telling me that if I wasn't pregnant we'd be having this same conversation about getting married when we barely know each other?"

He seemed to think about that and to Marti that meant *no*.

"It's the baby you really want," she said softly, sadly, surprised by just how sad it made her.

"That's absolutely not true—"

"You *don't* want the baby?"

"It's absolutely not true that the baby is the only thing I want or that if there was no baby, I wouldn't feel about this—about you—the way I do." He took a breath, slowing himself down before he went on. "I know that your relationship with Jack was the stuff fantasies are made of. I know this has all happened quick and backwards and probably isn't anybody's dream come true. But I *do* have feelings for you, Marti. And I think we have something here that's special all on its own. I think we can have something great together along with having a baby together, and I'm asking you to marry me, Marti. If, for you, it has to be because of the baby, then that's okay. Just marry me so we can make a life and a future together, so we can make the best of this."

He'd said that before, the night they were having pizza after seeing Hector that first time—they were talking about having doubts or regrets that there was a baby. Noah had said that the most important thing was for them to make the best of the situation.

And suddenly Marti couldn't help thinking that was part of what this was, too. And that Noah was saying whatever he thought he should say to convince her and bring it about.

And it just felt bad.

Jack had been devoted to her and her alone. Jack had adored her in a way that had left her never questioning it. Jack had told her—and everyone else—that he wanted more than anything to spend the rest of his life with her. Jack had proposed on one knee amid rose petals and candlelight and beautiful words about how much he loved her.

And now here she was, with Noah, who she thought was just putting a good face on things. Yes, he might have some feelings for her but she still thought this was more about the baby than about her. About him not losing another child.

And while she understood that, she didn't know why it was so hard to think that she wasn't the main attraction for him.

"No," she said. "I won't marry you."

His face fell. "Because I'm not that other guy," he said flatly. "But no one ever will be, Marti, and there are good things here with you and me."

"A marriage of convenience is not a good thing."

"It wouldn't be a marriage of convenience! Not for me!" he said, raising his voice slightly in what sounded like frustration.

But Marti just shook her head because no matter what he said, she still thought that was what he was proposing, a marriage he had to bring about so his rights to the baby were protected. And that wasn't a marriage she would agree to.

"Like I said, you can be as much a part of the baby's

life as you want to—I won't deny you that. But I also won't marry you."

Noah closed his eyes and shook his head. "I should have kept my mouth shut," he muttered.

Then he opened his eyes and said, "Please just think about it."

But Marti didn't need to think about it. The difference between what she'd had with Jack, between what had led up to almost marrying Jack, and this was so glaring to her she couldn't overlook it.

She swallowed the lump that had come into her throat—the lump she had no explanation for because she told herself that she shouldn't be so let down, so disappointed, so hurt...

"It'll be okay," she reassured Noah. "We don't have to be married for you to be this baby's dad. You *are* this baby's dad and nothing will ever change that. I give you my word."

"It isn't your word I want. It's you," Noah said fiercely.

Marti merely shook her head, denying him, denying his declaration.

But before he could say more, a big black sedan pulled into the driveway of Hector Tyson's house. Both Marti and Noah looked in that direction and despite the fact that the windows were too heavily tinted to see into the car, it was obvious that Hector had arrived home.

As the black sedan rolled slowly into the garage and the door automatically closed behind it, Marti turned back to Noah, finding his eyes on her again, dark and disturbed.

"If you don't want to go in with me, you don't have to," she said.

But Noah shook his head once again. "I told you, I'm not letting you anywhere near Hector alone."

Then Noah shoved off the side of his truck to stand tall and straight beside her and Marti was glad to have him there even if she had just rejected his proposal.

But going up to Hector Tyson's house as if her heart wasn't just a little bit broken all over again was one of the hardest things Marti had ever done.

Chapter Thirteen

"You two don't look happy to be here—have you come to say you were wrong and apologize to me?" Hector Tyson greeted Marti and Noah nastily when he opened his front door to them moments after Marti had refused Noah's proposal.

"Hardly," Noah answered.

"Then you aren't really welcome in my house," the old curmudgeon said, his hand still on the knob of the door that remained open with Marti and Noah barely inside of it. "I don't have to be hospitable to someone whose lawyer has sent me a letter telling me of her intention to sue me for restitution because she doesn't like the price her grandmother accepted for some land she sold me fifty-odd years ago."

"You may not have to be hospitable," Noah said, "but I'm here to make sure you talk to Marti."

Marti was trying to regroup, to dig her way out of the feelings that had washed over her in response to Noah's proposal. Feelings she couldn't quite fathom when it didn't seem as if disappointment and hurt should have been her reaction. What difference did it make if it had been a matter-of-fact, out-of-necessity proposal? It had come from someone she shouldn't have wanted a proposal from in the first place...

But at this particular moment she needed to be focused on Theresa, she reminded herself, and she did a fast snap out of her own problems, forcing herself to concentrate and recall what Hector had said about the lawsuit.

"It's more the principle than the price, Mr. Tyson," she said then. "You took a vulnerable, grieving seventeen-year-old girl into your home, isolated her, seduced her, got her pregnant and then used *that* to blackmail her into selling the land to you for a pittance of money. Then you got her to leave town, leaving the baby she had—*your* baby—to what? For you to *dispose* of somehow?"

Marti's own emotions had bubbled to the surface, fueling her anger.

"Who said I seduced Theresa or that she had a baby?" Hector challenged.

"Theresa told us, Hector," Noah said in a calmer but extremely serious tone, lending weight to what Marti had said even though some of it was only supposition.

"Nothing a crazy woman says means anything," the old man insisted with bravado.

"She told us about your affair with her," Noah continued with confidence that seemed genuine despite the fact that he was only outlining their assumptions and not actually stating facts. "She told us about the baby. And we've talked to Emmalina—we know Theresa went to Emmalina and the minister, that Theresa was pregnant when she did, that she took their advice to do whatever she had to do not to break up your marriage."

"Is Emmalina saying Theresa was pregnant by me?" Hector demanded. "Because no one has said anything like that to me all these years."

"Because they wouldn't," Noah claimed, without revealing that Emmalina didn't know for sure whether Theresa had been pregnant.

And since Noah had left Hector guessing, Marti chose that moment to push for more.

"We just want to know what happened to the baby."

Hector's eyes narrowed suspiciously. "I'm not admitting anything," he decreed. "But I'll tell you one thing—nobody gets anything from me unless I get what I want."

"Which would be what?" Marti asked.

"First of all, keep your Home-Max store out of my town. Secondly, no lawsuit is filed against me—not now, not ever. You Graysons will have to sign something binding from my lawyers to give up your right to ever sue me over that land in the future."

"Because you know they can win," Noah said.

"Nobody knows that," Hector countered. Then, aiming his attention at Marti, he said venomously, "But what I do know is that if you sue me, I'll drag your grandmother's name through the mud. I'll say things about her that will make you rue the day you ever opened this can of worms. I'll say she repaid my kindness to her by trying to destroy my marriage. By saying her baby—" He'd worked himself up into a frenzy and clearly that last part had come out on its own, because he stopped short.

"So there really was a baby," Marti said, somehow shocked all over again to have it confirmed. "A baby that you took from Gram. That's what she wants back—her son or daughter. That's what's so important to her, so important that she came all the way to Northbridge by herself."

"That's not what I said," Hector swore, as if that took back the words. "What I'm telling you is that I won't pay you people one red cent that doesn't get wrung out of me. And if it does, I'll make you sorry. But drop everything," he added as if he were baiting a hook, "and who knows what you might learn from me."

"Or we'll find out what we want to know some other way and still sue you and open a Home-Max here!" Marti said, so angry and so full of contempt on top of her own personal issues that she just couldn't maintain any control.

"I guess it's up to you," the old man sneered. "But if you want to take the easy way—the only way you're sure to get the information you want, the only way that'll save your grandmother from having everybody in town hear an ugly story about her—you'll drop the lawsuit and do what *I* want."

"You know, Hector, I always knew you were a bastard, but I never guessed you were this big a bastard," Noah said.

"You and everybody else around here," the old man countered. "It gives me less to lose because I don't care what any of you end up saying about me. But I'm betting your little girlfriend here cares what gets said about her precious lunatic grandmother and that gives me two aces in the hole—Theresa's reputation and that baby they want to know about."

Marti didn't think she could stay another minute and not throw something at the old man, so she merely turned and walked out.

"Always a pleasure, Hector," Noah said snidely as he followed her.

Marti kept on going to the curb, to the spot where Noah had so unromantically proposed and on to her brother's SUV. She got in behind the wheel, and Noah caught up with her as she was closing the door.

"Are you okay?" he asked.

Marti shook her head, but all she could say was, "I need some time to think."

Because the truth was, suddenly nothing seemed okay and she wasn't sure why.

It was as if just in the past half hour everything she'd thought she had a handle on had slipped out of her grip.

For her grandmother and for her.

* * *

"We're not going to take that!" Ry said over the phone late Sunday evening after Marti had told him what had gone on with Hector that afternoon. "That old buzzard can't get away with what he's done to Gram and call the shots, too."

She'd waited until Theresa and Mary Pat had gone to bed before calling Ry, because she hadn't wanted to take any chance that she'd be overheard.

"I'm not too sure how we're going to find the son or daughter that Gram had, though," she said.

"We'll just have to do what we can to dig up the truth on our own," Ry reasoned.

"And if we can't?"

"*Then* we'll talk about going through Tyson. And even if we have to do that, the lawsuit is the only flex-point, as far as I'm concerned. Home-Max goes in one way or another, so we can stick it to this guy on the business front, at least. But you stay away from him from here on," Ry said. "Let me or Wyatt deal with him. It sounds like he got to you."

"It's just been a bad day."

Following such a good night…

"Something else is going on." Ry was guessing, but he was so sure of himself that it came out as a state-ment of fact.

Marti debated about whether or not to tell her brother *what* else was going on. But everything would come out sooner or later—by breakfast this morning Theresa had already told Mary Pat that Marti was pregnant and that Noah was the father—and Marti needed to talk. So she did.

She told Ry everything, including that Noah was the baby's father and all the details of his proposal.

"And I just don't know why I care that it was so…so *practical*…"

Or why she'd been having such trouble keeping herself from crying since she got home from Hector's. But she certainly didn't want to start again now on the phone with her brother.

Who was chuckling slightly on the other end of the line.

"Could it be that what you really *care* about is Noah?" Ry asked.

"Care—as in *love?*" she said as if that were unthinkable.

"Not impossible, Marti," Ry said, interpreting her tone. "Look, Jack was The Man—you know we all thought of him as one of the family from when we were kids. Wyatt and I loved him like a brother. But he's gone. And as lousy as that is, it's a fact. Plain and simple. And you have to get on with your life. Especially now."

"Are you saying you think I should get married just because I'm pregnant, too?"

"Marti, no one—certainly not me—wants to see you make a lifelong calling out of being Jack's almost-widow. *Jack* would have hated that, and you know it. So you're pregnant by this other guy and you care enough about him to wish he hadn't asked you to marry him as if he were making a deal to buy a new car. All I'm saying is, maybe you should consider that there's a reason you slept with him in the first place and have been hanging out with him since you got to North-bridge—all reasons that don't have anything to do with the baby."

"But that is the reason I've been hanging out with him since I got here," she said out of contrariness when she knew better—the baby had only been an excuse, she'd wanted to see Noah. To go on seeing him...

"Don't try to feed me that," Ry countered. "If you didn't care about the guy, you wouldn't care *how* he proposed. And if you care about the guy, then maybe you should think about exactly what it is he's propos-ing. Especially when you sound so bummed out. This guy got under your skin, that seems pretty clear to me."

Okay, she knew it was futile to deny that any longer. To Ry or to herself.

"Besides," Ry went on. "Noah seems like a decent guy. Wyatt likes him. Gram and Mary Pat do, too. Maybe you should cut him some slack. From what you've said, I don't think that proposal was *all* about the baby, I just think that was the part you latched on to in order to give yourself the chance to ignore the rest. It sounds to me like he made that easy for you because he was a little afraid you'd reject him—probably because you're still focused on Jack."

"I am not."

"Oh, you *sooo* are. And if I were in Noah's shoes, that's what I'd be thinking—go with the baby angle because that has the best odds. Anything else runs up against that perfect lost love that nobody can beat."

Leave it to Ry to be blunt.

"It can't be beat with a let's-make-the-best-of-a-bad-situation proposal, that's for sure," Marti persisted.

"Like I said, if you didn't care about the guy you wouldn't care about the proposal. So maybe you need to let him know you *do* care."

And how was she supposed to accomplish that? Should she just hope her brother knew what he was talking about—that Noah might have feelings for her that he just wasn't saying much about—and go out onto that limb herself?

That didn't seem like the best idea she'd ever heard.

"I don't know…" she said, not willing to talk more about this with Ry. "I guess I'll have to think about it."

"Well, think about that instead of about Gram and Tyson and finding that baby from so long ago. I'll take over on that front, and you just work on your own problems."

Marti assured him she would. Then she changed the subject.

Finally they said good-night. And Marti was left sitting alone in her room wondering if her brother was right.

Did she care so much about the way Noah had proposed because she cared so much about Noah?

And had Noah used the baby as the main reason they should get married because it had seemed to carry more weight than he thought his feelings would?

Or were there just not many feelings on his part other than wanting to protect his rights to the baby?

Just as that thought put a damper on her spirits all

over again there was a knock on her bedroom window that startled her nearly to death.

Then she heard a hushed, "Marti!" from outside and she knew instantly that it was Noah.

She was dressed in what she'd intended to sleep in tonight—a cream-colored, lace-edged camisole that buttoned up the front and a pair of silky navy blue pajama pants. It was hardly accepting-company clothing, but Noah had seen her in much less, so she went to the window without covering up and opened the aged velvet drapes.

Sure enough, he was standing in the yard directly below the ledge, looking like a sexy cat burglar in jeans and a black turtleneck with the sleeves pushed to his elbows. His hair was tousled, and he was clean-shaven. Because she'd wanted some of the cool spring night air to come in, her window was open halfway and when she parted the curtains the scent of his cologne wafted in to her.

"What are you doing?" she said in greeting, not sure whether it was good or bad that a single glimpse of him gave her goose bumps.

"Come out," he instructed without answering her question.

"Or you could come in," she suggested, thinking fleetingly of the previous night that they'd spent in this room...

But Noah shook his head and merely said, "Come with me."

Of course he'd roused her curiosity, so Marti slid her feet into a pair of flip-flops and snatched a cardigan sweater to slip over her shoulders like a cape as she left her room and the house.

By then Noah was standing in the driveway on the passenger side of his truck with the door open.

"Get in."

"I'm not dressed to go anywhere—"

"You're fine. Just get in."

Marti got in. Noah went around the rear, hoisted himself behind the wheel and started the engine.

"I'm really not dressed," she said more insistently, but it didn't matter because before the words were completely out of her mouth he'd backed down the driveway and was headed away from the house.

Maybe they were going to his place to talk.

They certainly weren't going to talk now, she assumed, since Noah wasn't saying a word or looking anywhere but out the windshield as if he were alone.

"Where are we going?" she ventured as they passed the town square and the sleeping college.

"It's a secret," he allowed, reaching over to turn on the radio and effectively letting her know he didn't want any more said.

With her curiosity really roused now, Marti opted to just go along. Soon they'd driven onto Noah's property, past his house and barn and were going far out on a dirt road.

At such a distance from everything, the only illumination was moonlight, and just as Marti was about to demand to know what was going on, they came to a wooded area where Noah pulled to a stop and turned off the engine.

"I'll be right back," he said, getting out himself.

Marti lost sight of him in the darkness and through the trees until something sparked and suddenly there was a campfire burning in the distance.

Then Noah was back, opening the passenger door and holding out his hand for her to help her down from the truck.

"What are you doing?" she asked.

But Noah merely took her hand and urged her out so he could lead her to where he'd started the fire. A thick, downy quilt was laid out on the ground beside it, in a clearing surrounded by evergreen trees.

"Take a deep breath."

Marti complied, drinking in the strong scent of pine.

"What does it remind you of?" he asked. "The hotel in Denver?"

The hotel in Denver had been on the outskirts of the city, nestled in a rustic setting amid the same kind of fragrant evergreen trees. Fir logs, branches and bows had burned in the fireplaces in the lobby and restaurants, so inside and out the place had been scented with pine.

"Okay…" Marti agreed, "it smells like the hotel in Denver."

He still had hold of her hand and he took the other one, too, bringing her with him onto the quilt, into the golden glow of the fire that gilded his handsome features.

"Sit," he said when they were in the center of the quilt, sitting cross-legged himself and manipulating things so that she was, too, so that they were facing each other knees to knees.

"Now listen to me," Noah said in a voice that was soft and deep. "When we were in Denver there was nothing but you and me. We met and something combustible happened, something that no amount of good sense could keep us from acting on. There was nothing else then and—right here, right now—there's nothing but the two of us again."

So that's why they were out there.

"Somewhere along the way," he continued, "even though it wasn't my plan, something happened. I started thinking about you every minute of every day and every night. I started wanting to be with you constantly. I started putting everything in terms of you—it's you I want to be with at every meal, every time I'm walking down the street, when I'm at home or anywhere else. It's you I want to go to sleep with every night and wake up with every morning."

He squeezed her hands and tugged them slightly toward him.

"I fell in love with you, Marti," he said sincerely. "*You.* Just you. I know you can't say that same thing about—"

Marti pulled one hand out of his to press her fingertips to his mouth, to stop him before he said anything else.

Did he mean all he was saying or had he just had the chance to rethink where he'd gone wrong this afternoon?

She hoped she wasn't mistaken. It did seem as if he was speaking from the heart this time.

And when she considered who he was and what she'd come to know about him, it became less difficult to believe him. Because Noah was someone who had learned through pain and trouble to put effort into being exactly what Ry had said he was—a decent guy. He didn't lie. He didn't cheat. He didn't take the easy way out. He was a straight shooter. And she didn't think he would open his heart like this if he didn't mean it.

But now that it had come down to that, what about her? She'd just stopped Noah from saying that he knew she couldn't make those same declarations, that she didn't have those same feelings for him. But was that really true? Or was Ry right about that, too? *Did* she care for this man? More than care for him...

She was still looking into that chiseled face, her fingertips still staunching the flow of his words. His brows were creased with worry.

She thought of how many ways she'd discovered she liked Noah in the last week. Liked having him there for her when she'd had the heartburn and the dizzy spells, or to weather the storms with her grandmother and with Hector. She liked just being with him, talking to him, seeing him, hearing his voice.

She'd more than liked it all, she admitted to herself now. She'd craved Noah's company. And everything he'd said about how much he'd wanted to be with her was exactly how much she'd wanted to be with him. How much she'd just plain wanted him—his touch, his kiss, his body...

There weren't rose petals and wine and candlelight here. This wasn't Jack. But there was a roaring fire and a full moon and bright stars and the clean, clear scent of pine to bring her back to that first time she and Noah had been together, that first time when something bigger than both of them had been at work.

And while she might not recall much of their night together in Noah's hotel room in Denver, she did remember what had led up to it. The way Noah had made her feel even then—as if he saw the essence of her and her alone. There had been chemistry between them—they'd just clicked. And wasn't that what had happened again since she'd been in Northbridge?

It was. And it was something that didn't have anything to do with the baby. That really was just between the two of them. And if there was that much just between the two of them—before the baby and again since—then maybe what he'd said that afternoon about having something to build from, something other than the baby, was true.

Marti shook her head then and blinked back the tears that flooded her eyes when it struck her just how much she did care about this man.

"You *don't* know that I can't say that I love you," she whispered, shocked to find just how much she did.

Noah took her hand away from his face. "Does that mean you do?"

"This really doesn't have anything to do with the baby?" she asked rather than answer that, when a glimmer of doubt struck.

It was Noah who shook his head this time. "I trust that you wouldn't cut me off from my child. But *this*—" he brought her hands to his chest and held them there firmly "—you and me—is all this is about. If there wasn't a baby, I'd still be here, right now, telling you what I'm telling you and asking you to marry me because I don't want to be without *you*."

"I haven't heard you ask me anything," Marti pointed out.

"Marry me, Marti. Just because I want you and you alone. Marry me just because you want me. Marry me just because—maybe—you love me, too?"

She smiled. "The first part of that was supposed to be the question, not the last part."

Noah was still very solemn. "Seems like the last part is still a question, too, since I haven't heard it for sure."

Marti almost couldn't believe what she was about to say. "I never saw myself with anyone but Jack. I didn't think I could ever love anyone else. And I don't know how this happened—especially so fast and with so much…oomph. But I do love you, Noah. I do…" Her voice dwindled off in awe of her own feelings for him.

She saw his dark eyes fill the way hers had a moment before but he only smiled a devilish smile and said in a hushed voice, "It's about time. Nothing like leaving me hanging."

That made her laugh and kept tears from falling all the way around.

"So, *will* you marry me?" he asked.

"Yes," she answered simply because right there, right then, she honestly did know that he wasn't asking for any reason except that he wanted her. And because she wanted him, too.

Noah pulled her toward him and leaned in himself

to take her mouth with his in a kiss that was sweet and tender until passion overcame it.

His arms went around her and he raised them both to their knees so he could bring her in closer, so his hand could catch her head to cradle it when his lips parted, when his tongue came to claim hers, when that kiss deepened and turned all-consuming.

Marti's arms went around him, too; her hands found their way under his turtleneck to his broad, bare back.

Noah didn't need any more encouragement. The kiss eased up enough to put some space between them to accommodate his hands where they went to work on the buttons of her camisole as her sweater fell from her shoulders.

Big, strong, adept hands that had no problem with the tiny buttons before he slipped the camisole off and the cool night air brushed her naked breasts a moment before the warmth of his hands covered them.

But all too soon those hands were gone again, along with his mouth, so he could cross his arms over his flat belly, grab the hem of his shirt and yank it off over his head. Then it was the heat of his body meeting hers that chased away the chill as he laid them both down on the quilt and quickly disposed of the rest of their clothes.

They came together in a frenzy, starved for each other despite the fact that it had been only hours since the last time they'd made love. Exploring, learning, with hands and mouths and tongues, arousing every inch of flesh until they were both frantic with need that Noah met when he slipped inside of her.

The moan that escaped Marti was uncontrollable as together they began that quest for the climax that she knew Noah could take her to, the climax he reached a split second after she did, leaving them both breathless and satiated and spent.

Then they were lying there under the moon, under the stars and the treetops. Their legs were entwined, Marti's head was on Noah's chest and the fire was dancing beside them, bathing them in a soft golden glow and the whisper of warmth.

And that was when Noah said again, "I love you, Marti. More than you'll ever know."

"I love you, too, Noah," she responded.

"I'm thinking that we might not have had a crazy-long courtship like you had before, but that after this short one, we can have a nice long marriage. How would that be?"

She smiled in the darkness. "I'm counting on it."

"And I'm also thinking there'll probably be lots of kids just because I won't ever be able to keep my hands off you."

Marti laughed. "Okay. But let's just have this one to start with."

He hugged her tight. "Whatever you say." Then he kissed the top of her head and she could feel his breath hot in her hair as exhaustion seeped into them both.

And as she closed her eyes to give in to it, basking in the feeling of being in Noah's arms, of being against his naked body, of loving him so much it filled her almost to overflowing, Jack crossed her mind.

But nowhere in what she was feeling was there

guilt. Instead, in that instant, she knew that there was no cause for it.

For no reason she could know, she'd been offered another chance at the same kind of happiness she'd always thought she'd have with Jack. Only now she'd have it with Noah. Noah, who even Jack would have liked and approved of—she was sure of it.

And this time that happiness had come complete with a baby.

A baby that had brought them together. That would be the first that Noah could raise as his own. That had picked Marti up out of her grief and given her reason to go on.

And while the road to this moment had been entirely different with Noah than it had with Jack, Marti knew that what she'd found was no less perfect.

* * * * *

In honor of our 60th anniversary,
Harlequin® American Romance® is celebrating
by featuring an all-American male each month,
all year long with
MEN MADE IN AMERICA!
This June, we'll be featuring American men
living in the West.

Here's a sneak preview of
THE CHIEF RANGER by Rebecca Winters.

Chief Ranger Vance Rossiter has to confront the
sister of a man who died while under Vance's
watch…and also confront his attraction to her.

"Chief Ranger Rossiter?" The sight of the woman who'd stepped inside Vance's office brought him to his feet. "I'm Rachel Darrow. Your secretary said I should come right in."

"Please," he said, walking around his desk to shake her hand. At a glance he estimated she was in her mid-twenties. Her feminine curves did wonders for the pale blue T-shirt and jeans she was wearing. "Ranger Jarvis informed me there's a young boy with you."

The unfriendly expression in her beautiful green eyes caught him off guard. "Yes," was her clipped reply. "When we arrived in Yosemite the ranger told me I couldn't go anywhere in the park until I talked to you first."

"That's right."

"Knowing you wanted this meeting to be private, he offered to show my nephew around Headquarters."

So this woman was the victim's sister… "What's his name?"

"Nicky."

The boy who haunted Vance's dreams now had a name. "How old is he?"

"He turned six three weeks ago. Were you the man in charge when my brother and sister-in-law were killed?"

"Yes. To tell you I'm sorry for what happened couldn't begin to convey my feelings."

The woman's gaze didn't flicker. "I won't even try to describe mine. Just tell me one thing. Was their accident preventable?"

"Yes," he answered without hesitation.

"In other words, the people working under you fell asleep on your watch and two lives were snuffed out as a result."

Hearing it put like that, he had to set the record straight. "My staff had nothing to do with it. I, myself, could have prevented the loss of life."

Ms. Darrow's expression hardened. "So you admit culpability."

"Yes. I take full blame."

A look of pain crossed over her features. "You can just stand there and admit it?" Her cry echoed that of his own tortured soul.

"Yes." He sucked in his breath.

"I work for a cruise line. Aboard ship, it's the captain's responsibility to maintain rigid safety regulations. If a disaster like that had happened while he was in charge he would have been relieved of his command and never given another ship again."

Rachel Darrow couldn't know she was preaching to the converted. "If you've come to the park with the intention of bringing a lawsuit against me for negligence, maybe you should." It would only be what he deserved.

"Maybe I will."

In the next instant, she wheeled around and hurried out of his office. Vance could have gone after her, but it would cause a scene, something he was loath to do for a variety of reasons. In the first place, he needed to cool down before he approached her again.

The discovery of the Darrows' frozen bodies had affected every ranger in the park. A little boy had been orphaned—a boy whose aunt was all he had left.

* * * * *

Will Rachel allow Vance to explain—and will she let him into her heart?
Find out in
THE CHIEF RANGER
Available June 2009
from Harlequin® American Romance®.

We'll be spotlighting a different series every month throughout 2009 to celebrate our 60th anniversary.

Look for Harlequin® American Romance® in June!

Join us for a year-long celebration of the rugged American male! From cops to cowboys— Men Made in America has the hero you've been dreaming about!

Look for

The Chief Ranger

by Rebecca Winters, on sale in June!

Bachelor CEO by Michele Dunaway	July
The Rodeo Rider by Roxann Delaney	August
Doctor Daddy by Jacqueline Diamond	September

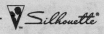
Silhouette®

SPECIAL EDITION

FROM *USA TODAY* BESTSELLING AUTHOR
MARIE FERRARELLA

THE ALASKANS

LOVING THE RIGHT BROTHER

When tragedy struck, Irena Yovich headed
back to Alaska to console her ex-boyfriend's
family. While there she began seeing his brother,
Brody Hayes, in a very different light. Things
were about to really heat up. Had she fallen
for the wrong brother?

*Available in June
wherever books are sold.*

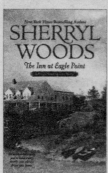  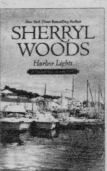

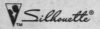

COMING NEXT MONTH
Available May 26, 2009

#1975 A BRAVO'S HONOR—Christine Rimmer
Bravo Family Ties
For more than a century, battling ranch families the Bravos and the Cabreras made the Hatfield and McCoy feud look like child's play. Until Mercy Cabrera fell for Luke Bravo, and their forbidden love tested the very limits of a Bravo's honor.

#1976 A FORTUNE WEDDING—Kristin Hardy
Fortunes of Texas: Return to Red Rock
It had been nearly twenty years since the one-night fling between Frannie Fortune and Roberto Mendoza. But now Roberto was back, and secrets of their past exploded into the present—along with an ironclad love that could not be denied.

#1977 LOVING THE RIGHT BROTHER—Marie Ferrarella
Famous Families
When tragedy struck, Irena Yovich headed back to Hades, Alaska, to console her ex-boyfriend's family—and began seeing his brother Brody Hayes, her best friend from high school, in a very different light. Things were really about to heat up in Hades….

#1978 LEXY'S LITTLE MATCHMAKER—Lynda Sandoval
Return to Troublesome Gulch
When the desperate boy called nine-one-one, little did EMS dispatcher Lexy Cabrera know that the little hero's father, Drew Kimball, whose life they saved that day, would turn around and heal *her*…with a love she'd all but given up on finding!

#1979 THE TYCOON'S PERFECT MATCH—Christine Wenger
The Hawkins Legacy
Brian Hawkins and Marigold Sherwood had spent summers at Hawk's Lake loving each other—until Mari moved away and a misunderstanding tore them apart. Now that CEO Mari was back in town, would all the old feelings come home to roost?

#1980 THE COWBOY'S SECOND CHANCE—Christyne Butler
Fate had not been kind to cowboy Landon Cartwright—loss and shame dogged his every step. But then he walked right into the arms of rancher and single mom Maggie Stevens…and a ray of light and love reached the very darkest spots of his soul.

SPECIAL EDITION